Looking for Georges Bizet
on Planet Heaven

Looking for Georges Bizet on Planet Heaven

Armineh Helen Ohanian

ISBN: 1508509794
ISBN 13: 9781508509790
Library of Congress Control Number: 2015902557
CreateSpace Independent Publishing Platform
North Charleston, South Carolina

If heaven exists, I wish it to be like my *Planet Heaven*.

Before dedicating my book to anybody, let me first explain the type of people on whom I wish to bestow this honor.

Imagine a mighty source of power created by the collective energy emanating from the mass of people with noble deeds. Furthermore, envision this swelling force transforming itself into a potent electrical reservoir. I would like to name it the Good Generator. In my imaginary world, there will be a constant exchange of powerful rays between this potent machine and God. Obviously, we can't have a Good Generator without an evil one. No need to say that the source of this latter reservoir would originate from the power flowing between the wicked people and the prince of darkness—Satan.

Since I love and support the Good Generator, and also for the purpose of further strengthening the might of goodness over the wicked force, I wish to dedicate *Looking for Georges Bizet on Planet Heaven* to all the lovely, sweet, fun-loving, open-minded, charitable, God-fearing, pure-hearted, good-tempered, funny, and optimistic people on earth (i.e., to the people belonging to the Good Generator).

Chapter 1

Mystery

A solemn chant resonated in the sanctuary as Virginia stroked the keys of the organ ever so softly. The parishioners seated in the pews surrounded by the overbearing walls of the redbrick church resembled a band of lifeless porcelain figurines. However, as soon as the organist started singing, they began shifting in their seats. Some sighed; others held handkerchiefs to their tearful eyes, while another few bent their heads in prayer.

Reverend Wright proceeded onto the pulpit through the side entrance. He looked dignified with his gray shimmering hair, a long pastoral robe, and a green stole draped around his neck. The pastor placed himself behind the podium and stared at the dark-brown wooden casket resting by the altar. He took in a deep breath and looked down sadly. The deceased was a friend.

As the pastor initiated the funeral service, Martha, a loyal member of the church, entered the building discreetly. She seemed like a floating ballerina as she proceeded smoothly toward the front row where her husband, Zaven, sat slouched over with his head drooping. Their son, Haroot; daughter, Sylvia; and their respective families surrounded him. To Martha, Zaven seemed somewhat peculiar. She did not remember ever seeing her husband hunched so dismally. Zaven generally held his body as upright as the tall red maple tree in their front yard. Today, he resembled the willow tree, which spilled its branches limply by the gate.

When Zaven finally looked up, Martha frowned, and exclaimed within, *what? It is not really like Zaven to appear unshaven in public.* Besides, Martha thought, on no occasion had she ever seen his eyes looking so ruby red and bloodshot. *Could he be upset about something?* she pondered. *I don't recall any unpleasant incident to have occurred!*

Martha sneaked like a wandering spirit to Zaven's side and nudged him to move over. She wished to sit next to her husband, hold his hand, and decipher the cause of his distress. Her heart simply broke to behold her dear husband's sad demeanor. Nevertheless, he appeared totally indifferent toward her. Martha shrugged, feeling hurt; she moved next to Sylvia and whispered in her ear, "Would you please make room for me?"

Surprisingly, Sylvia, too, disregarded her mother's request. *What is happening?* she wondered. Had she done something terribly wrong to offend them all?

Feeling despondent and dreadfully offended, Martha walked away and decided to stand aside. Anyway, with the pews fully occupied, there was no choice for her but to be on her feet. Besides, from her standing position, she could comfortably observe her family members and the congregation.

While Martha was thinking about her next move, she suddenly noticed Haroot wiping off a wayward tear as he draped an arm around his sad-faced father's shoulders. Martha stared at them all, totally shocked and lost in bewilderment. Martha, who, along with some latecomers, was leaning her body against the cold wall of the sanctuary, began wondering about the deceased. She asked herself if he or she had been a popular individual with lots of friends. The church was filled to the brim.

I don't remember having heard about any of the church members passing away, Martha told herself. She went to church almost every Sunday to meditate and get away from her whirlwind day-to-day life. She was in church for that very reason that day. Zaven was not a regular churchgoer like she was.

"Why don't you come to church with me one Sunday?" she had asked Zaven once.

"You know, Martha, I don't mind listening to sermons and the scripture readings. But what I really don't like about Sunday services are the boring religious rituals."

"What rituals?"

"You know, the usual hymn singings, the congregation reading the standard prayers and texts..." he said wearing a guilty look on his face. He didn't really mean to offend his wife.

"I understand. But such rituals—as you put it—don't bother me. For me, they are a part of my upbringing. Anyway, nobody is forcing you to go to church. I just thought it would be nice if you would keep me company from time to time," she added, smiling warmly.

The rest of her family members, like Zaven, merely showed up in church on special occasions such as Christmas candlelight services, christenings, weddings, and funerals. Therefore, she was puzzled about their presence in church that Sunday. When she left to go to church, Zaven, as usual, was busy watching his soccer game on TV. Maybe, while she had gone to pick up her prescription at the drug store before attending the Sunday service, Zaven had snuck out to go to church to surprise her. If so, then how about her two children and their families? And why was Zaven looking gloomy and sad? Was the deceased a friend of the family, she wondered? Then, how come she had no idea about it?

Yes, she desperately needed to know. Martha kept wondering and asking herself all sorts of questions. It was really a mystery!

Now, while standing by the sanctuary wall, Martha began daydreaming in spite of the funeral service. Suddenly, her life story set rolling like a motion picture in front of her eyes. Martha saw herself at twenty-one, meeting Zaven in Tehran at an American party. There were many US citizens working and living in Iran during the Shah's reign. Zaven had several American friends. So had Martha's Armenian friend, who had asked her to be his date at the party.

From the first moment Zaven set his eyes on Martha, he knew she was the girl of his dreams. Indeed, it was love at first sight. Martha was not smitten by Zaven at the start, although she found him to be very handsome. However, it didn't take her even a week to fall in love with that charming young man. As the saying goes, it was a match made in heaven. God had brought Zaven and Martha together. Who was there to separate them? In spite of some obstacles and difficulties, they got engaged within six months. Armenian culture requires for the betrothed to remain engaged for one full year, so they had to wait to get married. The logic behind the waiting period was based upon their belief that the two lovers would have ample time within that period to figure out whether they really were compatible. In those days, Armenian parents claimed that it would be wiser to break an engagement than to have a marriage result in a divorce.

Martha and Zaven's wedding took place on a steaming hot August night and was accompanied by a lot of singing, foot stamping, and fun. Within a year, God granted them a sweet and sprightly little girl whom they named Sylvia. She looked like a real doll with her curly brown hair, fair complexion, and glowing brown eyes. Their son, Haroot, was born three years later in Garmisch, Germany, where the US Army had transferred Zaven from Tehran. Back in Iran, Zaven had worked for the US Army Corps of Engineers.

At the funeral service that Sunday, Martha stared at her son and felt remorse for her past behavior as a young woman. *How could I have wanted to get rid of my adorable son when I realized I was pregnant with him?* Then Martha shook her head and told herself, *Shame on you, woman! Shame…shame…shame!*

In those days, Martha could not think of having many children. Indeed, she thought that taking care of one child was quite sufficient, especially since she worked full time at the US military base as a translator. Thus, to force a miscarriage, she lifted heavy objects and did everything in her power to lose her unborn child. Nevertheless, no matter how hard she tried, the baby held on. Of course, after the lovely baby was born, Martha was grateful that Haroot had clung to life and had made Sylvia the happiest sister on earth. Martha admitted that life would have been incomplete without their mischievous petite monsters—as she liked to call them—plotting naughty schemes together. Sylvia and Haroot were the best sister and brother that could exist.

The more Martha pondered her shameful past behavior, the more apprehensive she became. She wondered if God had tried to teach her a lesson by not allowing the unborn baby to die. Or maybe He had been kind to Martha and not wanted her to commit a sin. At the time, she had not thought that destroying the life of her unborn baby was the same as committing an act of murder. Martha wondered how certain women who had gone through abortion felt after losing their babies.

Chapter 2

Married Life

Being swamped by memories of her youth, Martha could not concentrate on the church service. By now, it was clear to her that she was more interested to travel back to her past life than to follow the tedious rituals of the funeral ceremony. Thus, she let her mind continue drifting around like a graceful, wide-winged seagull floating in the bright-blue sky.

Martha recollected that all through their married life, she and Zaven had led an eventful and exciting existence. The couple and their two children had toured some interesting places in diverse parts of the world. They had also lived in several fascinating countries. A few times, they had returned to Iran, where Martha, Zaven, and Sylvia had been born, but not for long. The last time they left Iran was right before Ayatollah Khomeini's terrible regime.

Yes, all through those years, life for them—as for many married couples—was packed with love and happiness intertwined with the usual tribulations, snags, and hitches. Fortunately, the older Zaven and Martha grew, the more they enjoyed a harmonious time together and appreciated each other.

No wonder that on this specific day, Martha felt offended and dejected. She could not comprehend the frosty behavior of her husband and two children. Indeed, what had she done to deserve such cold treatment?

Martha sighed. Then, she craned her neck from where she was standing and stared at the casket.

Suddenly, Martha felt baffled. She was dazed and totally lost. Why did she feel so strange? She rubbed her eyes and shook her head in bewilderment. *Is this a dream?* she mused. To her great astonishment, Martha realized that she could see through the closed wooden box. *How strange*, she told herself. *How can a coffin lid be see-through?*

From her vantage point, Martha could get a glimpse of the misty shape of a dead woman lying cold inside the coffin. However, before she had a chance to take a closer look, the booming chant of the congregation singing the hymn "This Is My Song" froze her solidly in place. She sighed and took a long, deep breath. This was the same hymn that they had sung at her father's funeral when she was only eight and a half years old. Martha began weeping silently. The pain of losing her father as a little girl had never left her, even at old age.

Martha wished she had a hymnbook to join in singing with the crowd. However, even if she had a chance to look for one, there would be none to be found. The pews were all occupied by a large multitude of people, most of whom she recognized. Thus, not knowing the words by heart, Martha simply settled for humming along. A painful lump began forming in her throat, making it impossible for her to continue.

At long last, when the congregation ceased singing, Pastor Wright started with his second scripture reading. Then he began with the sermon.

Meanwhile, Martha continued examining the cadaver from her standing position. Indeed, her strange ability to see through the top of the casket bemused her.

It did not take Martha long to figure out the identity of the deceased. And as she finally managed to view the mysterious cadaver, her jaw dropped, and her eyes popped wide open with shock and terror. "Oh, Lord!" she gasped. "No, this can't be true! It's not possible!"

Chapter 3

The Sad Revelation

Martha crouched upon the steps leading to the altar and rocked her body from side to side, feeling totally confused. Presently, as the pastor continued with the sermon, people dug their heads once again into their hymnbooks and began singing another sad hymn. In the meantime, Martha realized that she was free to act as she wished. It became obvious that no one had noticed anything about her presence or her actions.

The singing soared higher and higher, pounding like a drum into Martha's head. She felt faint and heavy hearted. Her temples throbbed, her heart thumped madly, her ears rang like the chimes of a grandfather clock, and her head began spinning as if she were riding a carousel or a roller coaster. Martha felt tipsy and dizzy at the same time, just like those instances when, after having had a few drinks, Martha would lie down to sleep, and the ceiling would give the impression of whirling fiercely above her head. Nevertheless, despite her anguish, she felt extremely light, as light as a feather that pops out of a pillow and floats about in the air with the slightest breeze.

Martha shook her head in disbelief and heard herself crying out, almost yelling, "When did I die? How come I don't remember anything?"

At first, Martha could not recall anything and didn't even know how she had died. Suddenly, it dawned on her. "Of course!" she said. "Now I know."

It had to do with Martha's back. She remembered that eighteen years earlier a well-known neurosurgeon had operated on her back. Then, three years later, Martha had had a severe neck surgery. Right before her death, she needed to go for another back surgery, which caused Martha her life on the operating table.

Sitting there near the casket, Martha reached back to touch her spine to see if she could feel any pain, but to her great amazement, she felt nothing at all.

Scrambling to her feet, Martha once more glanced glumly at her own dead face. It looked as calm and lifeless as the smooth surface of a lake. Martha's hair was colored in golden brown with light streaks. Her closed eyes were slightly slanted, and her eyebrows were dark and curved. So were her eyelashes, despite her age. Thanks to the organic coconut oil she rubbed in every night–a little secret she loved to share with older women.

Facing the congregation, Martha called out, "Listen, everybody, this woman lying dead in the coffin is by no means me." She wiped her tears and continued. "Look up. Look around you. Right here, to your right. Now to your left. There...there. Do you see me?"

Indeed, Martha could not bring herself to accept that that cold, motionless figure resting in the casket could be her real self. She felt very much alive. She sighed and recalled how she always had desired and tried to be an elegant, good-looking woman, right up to the very last moment. Indeed, all through her life—even as an aging woman—she thought she should try her best to look trendy. What's more, she had worked out and played tennis regularly in order to keep her body in a good shape. Martha often mentioned to her friends that at their age, it was imperative for them to look their best. She had said, "Elegance is one of the most important assets of our life at old age. By being stylish and chic, at least when we look in the mirror, we can proudly tell ourselves that we are presentable and well put together."

Martha loved it when people complimented her. She despised when certain individuals kept mentioning how petite and slim she had become. She already was aware of her loss of height and weight and did not need to be constantly reminded of it. Maybe some women would take such comments as complements. However not Martha.

One day, as she was having lunch with her good friend Gitta, the conversation somehow circled around that same subject. Martha told Gitta that in her mind, she always remained that special young girl who used to be pretty and fun loving. "I don't need to look at a real mirror," she told her friend. "All I need to do is to look inside into my inner mirror."

Gitta said jokingly, "What do you see? Don't tell me virtue and goodness. That's boring!"

"I'm saying no such thing. No, ma'am! What I'm talking about is that when I look into my inside mirror, I still see a young, exciting, and pretty woman—the same one who stole Zaven's heart the first moment he set his eyes upon her."

"That's my girl! Yes, just like me. I see myself as that young and pretty person that I used to be," Gitta said.

Martha laughed and told her friend, "Yes, as I said, I feel exactly the same as you do. It's only when I stand in front of an actual mirror and gaze at my wrinkles that reality stares me back in the face."

Gitta giggled like a young girl. "Stop! Don't make me think of my own marks of beauty!"

Martha smiled mischievously and added, "Well, there's nothing we can do about those damn wrinkles—or 'marks of beauty,' as you call them. Unless we decide to go for Botox or plastic surgery and look ridiculous…"

"Yes, like some old or even young women who look exactly the same, with their puffed-up faces and lips?"

Martha nodded. "Exactly! What's more, they look ridiculously artificial! I sometimes ask myself, 'Don't they see themselves in the mirror? Can't they tell that they look nothing like before?'"

Gitta said, "I know. They all look as if they have popped out of the same mold or machine!"

The two friends burst out laughing as they imagined themselves being as one of those puffy-faced women.

"Whatever!" Gitta said, wiping her tears of laughter.

Martha rubbed her chin, stared Gitta in the eyes, and said, "Another thing that I find to be important is for us not to forget to live a happy life. I personally believe that the remainder of my life should be a joyous one."

"No doubt about it," Gitta answered. "Come on, tell me how."

"I don't know. All I think is that we should love every moment of our lives, no matter under what condition. Yes, we must try to make life pleasant and rich." Martha laughed and added, "As rich and majestic as, for example, Beethoven's Seventh Symphony."

Each time Martha listened to that symphony, she felt uplifted, as if it were the richest and fullest time of her life.

Gitta shook her head, not understanding what Martha really meant. "You are crazy! And, that's what I like about you. Honestly, who would think of comparing the richness of life to Beethoven's Seventh Symphony?"

Chapter 4

Still at Church

When Martha remembered that she was indeed dead, she heaved a sigh of desperation and said, "Now I understand what's going on! For a second, when I approached my family members, I thought they no longer cared about me."

Then, she laughed and went on saying, "How funny! None of them have any clue that I'm right here and that a few minutes ago I was standing by their side."

Martha gazed at Zaven, and for a second, she perceived him as the young fellow she used to know during her youth. He was tall, slim, and very handsome. He wore a crooked smile on his face and had bright, blue-green eyes. She grinned, remembering the past. Drifting toward her husband, Martha sat on his lap. She kissed him on the lips and whispered into his ear, "You know what, my love? I must admit that although you were a handsome fellow in the old days, today I find you even more attractive with your graying hair."

Zaven shifted on his seat. Martha believed that he, too, might be experiencing some memories of the old days.

Alternatively, he might be feeling her presence. She smiled with contentment.

Suddenly, Martha felt like being her old, clownish self and bumped Zaven on the head. "Hey, stupid! I'm right here, sitting in your lap!"

Then she stared at his sad face and told herself, *I think he misses me a lot.*

Martha began tickling him and for a minute forgot that she was dead. "Hey, man, cheer up!"

When she did not perceive any change in his mood, she told herself, *Let me think of a funny story to remind him about.*

Martha creased her brow and tried to recall an amusing incident from the past. As she kept on digging into her memory, she suddenly blurted out, "Hey, do you remember when we were visiting India, and we went to the fortune teller at the hotel?"

Zaven didn't budge an inch. He simply sat there limply, looking depressed.

At the time of their visit to India, they had been living in France in the city of Annemasse. One day a few days before their journey to India—when Zaven and Martha were strolling along the Main Street in Annemasse—a gypsy woman approached them and began nudging Martha. "Let me read your palm. I am one of the best fortune tellers among the gypsies."

Martha answered nonchalantly, "No, thank you."

The woman insisted. "You'll regret it!"

Martha simply shrugged and dismissed her. The gypsy gripped Martha's hand and forced it open. She thrust a swift glance at her palm and declared loudly with venom, "In two days, you'll be struck by a car and killed."

Zaven was extremely disturbed by those unwelcome comments and glared at the gypsy. But Martha just laughed and told her husband, "Don't worry—she said those words out of spite. I guess you noticed how angry she looked when I refused to let her read my palm?"

The following day, they had traveled to India. In Kolkata, after their arrival, the first thing Zaven suggested was, "Hey, Martha. I have noticed that there is a fortune teller at the hotel. I want us to check it out."

Martha accepted reluctantly. She was well aware that Zaven was still apprehensive about the stupid gypsy's prediction about her fate and wanted to see what the hotel fortune teller had to say.

A smiling fellow wearing a turban and traditional Indian costume opened the door to a dark room. He shook his head from shoulder to shoulder, like Indian female dancers do, said hello, and let Martha and Zaven into the incense-infused room. The moment they sat on two high stools in the spooky room, with its curtains tightly drawn, the guy began rambling something. He continued babbling in a strange accent that sounded more like Urdu. They both concentrated hard in vain to understand what he was saying. All they could capture from his words was the refrain that he repeated at the end of each paragraph: "Kissy-kissy, lovey-dovey."

Back at the funeral, Martha kissed Zaven's cheek and said, "Hey, kissy-kissy, lovey-dovey. Cheer up man!"

Then, she walked to the altar, where her casket lay. As she floated forward, once again she was overwhelmed by desperation and sorrow. Martha had no idea how long she would be wandering on Earth before moving on to a different dimension of existence. Indeed, she really had no idea what was in store for her. Would she be roaming around her husband and family members for an unknown period of time? Martha had read a while back about spirits lingering on Earth because they could not find their way onto the world of the spirits, or as some people would like to call it, toward Heaven.

Chapter 5

Lost and Lonely

Sitting on the steps leading to the altar, Martha looked at Zaven from far and addressed him, "Well, I guess I'll have no choice but to leave you forever. Oh, dear—how I'm going to miss you!" Then, turning her attention to the rest of her family members, she suddenly felt an inexplicable sorrow. The thought of also leaving them behind for good distressed her immensely. "How is this possible?" Martha wailed, as tears flowed down her cheeks and streamed all over her neck. Soon, she got upon her feet and rested her body against the wall by the altar.

She gazed at her daughter-in-law, Jenik. At forty-nine, Jenik was as beautiful as ever. Martha remembered the good times they had had together during their shopping jaunts. They would enter a department store in Manhattan at midday, and leave the store at dusk with loads of shopping bags. Haroot seated between Jenik and Zaven, looked as handsome as his father with his graying hair. As for Sylvia, to her mother, she was the prettiest, warmest, and the most compassionate daughter anyone could ask for. Next, Martha gazed at Hilda, her gorgeous twenty-two-year-old granddaughter—Jenik and Haroot's eldest daughter—who was studying psychology. Martha and Hilda had a special relationship together. Since Hilda's elementary school years, the two had enjoyed sharing interesting books together. And then there was the loving and friendly Alenoosh, Haroot's younger daughter. She was a stunning twenty-year-old. Alenoosh was studying to become a fashion designer and a businesswoman. Alain, their attractive eighteen-year-old brother, was a talented, artistic young fellow. He was planning to become an actor as well as a clothes designer like Alenoosh. Alain, ever since his childhood had been a good friend of Martha's. Sylvia's son, Leon, was also a fine-looking fellow. He was thirteen and a brilliant student at Westhampton Beach Middle School. Leon was very loving. He always hugged his grandparents compassionately, with love radiating through his whole being. Leon not only was a bright and hardworking student, but he was also a talented soccer star. Martha was very proud of her grandchildren, and seeing them all at church on the day of her funeral filled her with a mixture of sadness and pleasure.

Next to Sylvia sat Igor, Sylvia's pleasant husband. He looked calm and collected. Martha remembered how Igor brought beautiful roses and tulips for her from time-to-time. She smiled and said, "I think he is going to miss me. Martha also saw Jenik's tall and slim brother, Viken, and his wife, Sabina, present among the family members. They, too, were already missing Martha. The couple used to have thought-provoking conversations with Martha and Zaven about books and other interesting subjects.

Martha glanced at all of them with great sorrow. Yes, she did not at all feel content parting with them. *Why do people have to die at all?* She pondered. *Or, if they had to, couldn't they all leave Earth together?* Turning her attention to Zaven again, she uttered, "I wish you were coming with me to wherever I'm headed." She sobbed bitterly and continued, "I don't want to leave. No, I really don't..."

It is true that during her youth, there were times when Martha disagreed with her husband. Often, she found herself not having much freedom in the management of their household. Zaven used to inspect everything, including the refrigerator, her paperwork, filing, and even her closet. When she was young, she used to get upset. However, as they reached their sixties, they began being more lenient with each other. What mattered most was that they loved each other dearly. Moreover, toward the end of her life, Martha was to a great extent dependent upon her husband. Yes, she could never imagine life without him. Now, she was totally on her own. Who would drive her around? With whom could she talk about her problems, or joke and laugh?

Chapter 6

A Pleasant Surprise

The lifeless figure resting in the coffin looked like a total stranger to Martha. She told herself, *that weird person lying there like a piece of dry lumber could by no means be me.* But who was she supposed to be, now that she was no longer the same character? She was indeed confused as her spirit floated about aimlessly. "Oh, Lord, I am going through a crazy phase! I really feel like dying," she whimpered, then laughed hard, reminding herself that she was already dead. "OK, I know. I have to go away to somewhere unknown and leave my family behind, but dear Lord, help me. Where, and how? Really, I'm totally lost. There's no way I can idle around like this forever!"

As Martha drifted about feebly, feeling weightless and muddled, suddenly, she was overcome by a strange sensation. Martha felt some unusual activity going on in the air, as a blurry spirit began shifting around like a drifting cloud a few steps away. Martha narrowed her eyes in puzzlement as she beheld a figure gradually taking shape not too far from the pastor.

"Goodness!" Martha was flabbergasted. "Am I dreaming?"

She rubbed her eyes and squinted to perceive her surroundings clearer. Yes, indeed, to her great astonishment, standing by the altar was her darling Uncle Sooren, whom she had lost to bone cancer more than thirty-five years back. He was barely fifty-five when he passed away.

"Hello, Martha," he uttered, beaming warmly. "It's me."

Martha was speechless. She couldn't wait to find out what the next step was going to be. *Is he here to help me?* She wondered.

Martha rushed toward Sooren with her arms opened wide and hugged him hard. Then, overcome by extreme emotion, Martha began to sob loudly. "Oh dear...oh dear! I'm so grateful to you. Really...I can't thank you enough for coming to my rescue!"

"It is my pleasure, dear Martha. I'm well aware how scared and lost you might feel. But don't be afraid, my darling niece. I'm here to assist you on your long journey home."

Martha stood at the tip of her toes to be able to wrap her arms around her beloved uncle's neck. "I really can't believe my luck!" she blurted out, showering him with kisses. "I thought I was dead and all by myself. I really had no idea what was in store for me."

Sooren nodded compassionately and gave her a broad, warm smile. From her uncle's demeanor Martha could tell how much he had missed her. She could also guess that he understood her niece's desolation.

Martha and Uncle Sooren used to be good friends when Martha was a teenager. She recalled how he'd allowed her at eighteen to have one or two small shots of vodka with him. Having grown up without a father, Martha considered

Sooren as a father figure, as well as a friend. Her uncle, in turn, wanted Martha to be sincere with him about everything she did. He thought that by allowing her to have a drink with him and other family members, she would not try to be mischievous at different gatherings with her friends. He was aware of how young kids drank and smoked when they attended parties. Even the strict rules imposed by their Armenian parents were not enough to restrain the youth from wrongdoing.

Not only was Martha close to her uncle, but she also had a good relationship with her modern and progressive-minded mother. In reality, Martha was friends with everybody in the family. They included her loving sister, Lily, and her intellectual third brother, Arek; her second brother, Armen, the most charming, charismatic, and fun person; and her eldest brother, Artash, who showered his youngest sister with complete adoration. Who could ask for a warmer and more caring family than hers?

Thus, even after her death, Martha felt blessed to have her uncle by her side. "Oh, thank God! I'm so happy to have you with me. It's wonderful! I don't feel lost anymore," she said.

Sooren patted Martha on the shoulder as she added, "Do you have any idea how much I've missed you all these years?"

He nodded. Martha hugged him once again, beseeching him, "So, Uncle Sooren, am I really...really dead?"

"Yes, my darling Martha, you are really...really dead. I am sure you have already seen your deceased body lying in the casket."

Martha didn't respond. The thought of her dead body somewhat disturbed her. In fact, she had no desire to associate herself with it. As far as Martha was concerned, she still existed. That dead figure had nothing to do with her. Looking at the nonexistent Martha lying motionless in the coffin angered her immensely.

Sooren looked at Martha with great concern and said, "I know how aggravating it is for you to discover that you're dead, but don't worry. You will soon get used to the feeling."

"I'm sure I will, especially now that I have you helping me. Indeed, I'm not alone anymore, and that's what matters."

Sooren appeared pleased. Staring at his niece lovingly, he asked, "Now, tell me something. You don't feel pain anymore, do you?"

Martha turned her head to the right and left to figure out whether she could move her neck with ease. Contrary to her living days, Martha had no problem in doing so. She then bent down and straightened her body with ease.

"You know, Uncle," Martha said, rather than answering her uncle's question directly, "I can never forget how Zaven took care of me after both surgeries."

"Did he?"

"Absolutely. Especially after my neck surgery, when I had to wear a body brace night and day for a full year."

Sooren nodded approvingly. "Anyway, I'm happy that all your problems are left behind, and as I can detect, you have no pain."

Martha beamed, shook her head, and uttered with gleaming eyes, "No. Uncle, I have zero pains! It feels that, like a car, I am fully repaired. Yes, Uncle, I am totally renewed. Besides, I feel weightless and extremely relaxed."

"That's good. That's very good," Uncle Sooren said. "I know exactly how wonderful it feels to be pain-free after suffering for such a long time. I've been there myself."

Chapter 7

The Dream

Martha listened intently to Sooren as he spoke to her about how great he felt after his death. His conversation made Martha think of an interesting dream she had a while back, concerning the same subject regarding her uncle.

The year was 1994, and Zaven and Martha were living in St. Petersburg. Their daughter and son by then were grown up and attending college in New York. Zaven's American company had transferred him to head their branch in the Soviet Union, where they ended up living for about a year. Yes, Martha and her family were real Globetrotters! Since leaving Iran – after the Iranian revolution – they had resided in many countries. Prior to their move to St. Petersburg, they first lived in New York for nine years, and then in London for another two years.

One night, when Zaven was away in Ukraine on business, Martha had a pleasant dream. She dreamed that they lived in an unknown land where their house was located on top of a hill across a broad, open field. The landscape somehow resembled a beautiful green, hilly Iranian site. In her dream, as Martha was busy cooking in the kitchen, she heard a voice calling out her name: "Martha…Martha…"

Martha ran outside, raising her head to look at the cloudless, brilliant sky. Then she stared at the green fields down below. She wondered where the voice emanated from.

"Martha!" she heard the person calling again. The voice sounded familiar. Martha looked straight ahead at the opposite hill some distance away and noticed the blurry figure of a man perched against the sun's bright rays. Martha used her hand like a visor to shield her eyes to have a clearer view of the individual in question. To her great amazement, she discovered the person to be her Uncle Sooren, who had died a few years earlier.

Martha yelled out loud, to make herself understood on the opposite side, "Is that you, Uncle Sooren?"

"Yes," the answer came back loud and clear. "I've come to visit you."

"Come on over. I am preparing some food. Let's have lunch together."

In no time, Sooren appeared beside her. He did not seem to have changed at all. In fact, he looked exactly the same as Martha had known him as a child, with the same sweet smile that made his dark eyes turn into two twinkly, lively slits when he laughed.

Martha invited her uncle to take a seat, and while setting the table, she pelted him with all kinds of questions.

"How's life in Heaven?"

"Very good," he answered.

"Please, tell me more."

"Well," he said, "we have two options in Heaven. One choice is that you can decide that you will be eating food. The other way is not to eat at all."

Martha asked Sooren about the significance of those two types of lives.

He collapsed comfortably onto the sofa, taking off his sneakers, and said, "Those who choose to eat eventually get sick and die again in Heaven. However, if you seek everlasting life, you simply don't eat."

Martha smiled at him, still extremely happy to have her lovely uncle visiting her. She said, "Uncle Sooren, please don't bother to tell me which option you chose when you entered Heaven. I already know."

He sighed. "Yes, you know how much I love good food and vodka, don't you?"

"Oh, goodness, it wasn't difficult to guess that you would choose the first option!"

"Yup, and I'm already sick."

"I'm sorry!" Martha said. Then, changing the subject she continued, "Uncle Sooren, do you know that I often think of you?"

"I know you do. That's why I've come to see you."

After lunch, he had hugged his niece hard and vanished into thin air.

Chapter 8

Good Old Friends

Back at the church, Martha looked around, and her eyes rested upon dear Angelica and her husband, Jimmy. She had met Angelica at the same time as Michele, Marlin, and Patricia more than twenty years earlier when they had first moved to Westhampton. Yes, Martha told herself that she was blessed to have so many great friends. She felt dizzy again. She rubbed her eyes to give them some rest. Martha couldn't believe her eyes. There were even more friends present! There were Mary, Suzy, Connie, Jeanette, Janna, Louisa, and dear Gitta, a pal of many, many years. She couldn't really count anymore. "My goodness!" Martha exclaimed. "I hadn't realized what a privileged woman I used to be! Now it is good-bye to them all."

Martha rushed forward hugged and kissed all her friends one by one. Then, as she began parting, she turned back and waved at them for the last time, and said, "Bye, my lovely friends. No more fun lunch gatherings. No more birthday celebrations. Yes, it is farewell forever!"

Chapter 9

A True Friend

While waving good-bye one more time to her friends, Martha fixed her gaze on Michele and thought of a very special day, a day that made her aware of a pleasing reality.

It was a glorious spring morning, and Martha was in one of her cheerful moods. She was going to play tennis with her three favorite friends, Michele, Marie, and Marcia. They were known at the Sunshine Health Club in East Quogue as the Four Musketeers. Their tennis game was scheduled for Fridays. After the game, they always went to Jane's Restaurant for lunch in Westhampton Beach. It was so much fun.

That day, Martha had opened the front door singing away joyfully, tennis racket in hand, and prepared to walk to her car. She had hardly taken a step outside when suddenly, she froze in place. She immediately rushed back into the house, closed the door, and slumped into the armchair in the hall. She was distressed. Martha just sat there for a while, holding her head between her hands in desperation.

"Oh no!" She panicked. "Why do these things always happen to me?"

The problem was a dead mouse in her driveway. Martha was not as scared of snakes as she was of mice. Something must have happened to her as a little girl to have made her so fearful of those little, creepy rodents. With her bad luck, she always seemed to come across one or be the first person to spot one. Just last September, Martha and her husband were waiting in Manhattan at a garage for the attendant to bring their car when Martha noticed a mouse zooming by at the speed of lightning. She yelled and turned her head to avoid looking at it. Of course, Zaven immediately could tell the reason for her anguish. He was well familiar with her mouse yells. Meanwhile, other people waiting for their cars to arrive looked at Martha sideways, possibly thinking she was crazy. Naturally, they did not see the mouse. Yes, Martha always was the unlucky person who had to see those horrifying, speedy creatures.

Well, maybe tennis was out for Martha that day. She thought that she had no choice but to stay at home and wait until evening for Zaven to return and help her with her dilemma. However, giving it a second thought, she realized that it would be very selfish of her to opt out of the tennis game at the last moment. It would create a problem for her friends, who were counting on her to be their fourth player. Indeed, she would be spoiling their game and also their lunch. So, what was she supposed to do?

Martha definitely was not going to pass by the dead mouse in order to get into her car. Nevertheless, she tried very hard to convince herself to venture out of the house, with no success. To make matters worse, Martha felt nauseated. Each time that she saw a mouse, she felt like throwing up. In those days, Martha did not have a cat, but even if she had one, she didn't think she could use a cat to save her from her misery. Eating a dead mouse could be the end for a cat. Often mice die because of ingesting poison left out for them. So, what was Martha supposed to do? How could she get herself to the health club from her home in Westhampton?

Martha kept on thinking of a solution as she paced the length of the hall at least fifty times, the scary image of the dead mouse engraved in her mind

Suddenly, she heard herself saying loudly, "But of course, I know what to do. I should shade the left side of my face with my left hand in order to block the sight of the mouse from my sight!"

Martha smiled triumphantly, happy for having finally solved that terrible impasse. So that's exactly what she did. Then Martha scurried into the car and drove away as fast as she could.

After the game was over, before going out for lunch, Martha turned to Michele and said, "My lovely Michele, I have a big favor to ask you."

"What's wrong?"

Martha answered, smiling bashfully, "There's a dead mouse in my driveway."

"So?"

Martha bit her lower lip with embarrassment. "Do you think you could follow me to our house in your car, before we go for lunch, and get rid of it for me?"

Suddenly, Michele's smile faded away. Her face dropped. She looked really pale, and her eyes lost their luster. She answered Martha with a cold tone of voice, "OK. My friend, I'll do as you say."

Before they drove away from the sport club, Martha wondered about Michele's sudden change of expression. She asked herself if she was mad at her for having asked for a favor. However, that was not like Michele. She was such a kind person.

They entered the driveway and got out of their cars. This time, Martha shielded the right side of her face, in order to block the view of the dead creature, as she rushed toward the house. She dashed to the garage, where a broom, dustpan, and a garbage canister lay. Picking up the broom and the dustpan, Martha passed them on to Michele with her eyes closed, then turned her head away to avoid seeing her friend scoop up the mouse. She heard Michele yelling and crying out with fear and disgust.

"Oh dear," Martha called out. "Don't tell me you are scared of mice, too!"

"I am horrified," she answered, "but I couldn't refuse you when you came to me for help."

"I'm so sorry. I'm really sorry." Martha kept repeating, as Michele dumped the mouse in the garbage can and shut the lid.

Michele then sighed with relief. "You know what, my friend?"

"I'm listening. Do tell me, please," Martha said.

"The fact that you came to me and not to the others for help with your problem means a lot to me."

Martha flashed a warm smile to Michele as she hugged her hard. She wished to thank her for her heroism, telling herself, *What do you call my lovely friend's brave action, if not total devotion and loyalty?*

Chapter 10

Eulogy

Walking back toward the altar to join her uncle, after saying good-bye to her friends, Martha suddenly had to stop and listen to the pastor. He was inviting her family members to say a few words about their beloved wife, mother, and grandmother. Zaven remained motionless while the rest of the family members got up and each said a loving word or two about her.

Alenoosh stood behind the pulpit and said, "I had a cool grandmother. She loved to have fun. Once I told her that at her funeral, I would not cry. I knew she wouldn't like it if I did. Instead, I said to her that I would dance around her coffin." Alenoosh waited for a while, and then swallowed, coughed, and cleared her throat before continuing. "Of course, I'm not going to dance here at the sanctuary."

At this point, she had to stop in order to give the congregation a chance to finish their laughter. She added, "But when we go to the restaurant to celebrate my grandma's life, I'll make sure we have some music playing, so that I can get up and dance to fulfill my promise." Alenoosh sighed, swallowed the lump in her throat, looked down to hide her tears, and carried on, "I must admit that I already miss my grandmother, my friend so badly!" Then, having finished her words, she rushed back to her seat as fast as she could.

Before the funeral service ended, the pastor added a few extra words. He stressed that Martha once mentioned to him that the main reason she loved Jesus was because of his teachings particularly, those concerning love. Therefore, that day the theme of the sermon was love.

That was absolutely true. Martha did believe in the type of love taught by Jesus. During the days when Martha, Zaven, Haroot, and Sylvia temporarily moved back to Tehran from Geneva—where they had been living for ten years—an incident took place that confirmed the pastor's words.

As Martha listened to the pastor's comments, she nodded approvingly and remembered their time in Tehran.

In 1975, Zaven's company had transferred him to Tehran on a temporary assignment. This took place a couple of years prior to the Iranian Islamic revolution.

Martha signed a contract there to work with a temporary job–placement agency. The agency used to send Martha to perform secretarial and administrative tasks at different establishments. On one occasion, she went to work for a German corporation, where an office boy called Hussein used to serve tea to the employees and drop off documents and mail. Hussein liked to evangelize Islam to Martha. For some reason, Hussein thought she would be a good candidate to convert. Hussein kept sermonizing about Mohammed's might in beheading his enemies and forcing different nations—such as Iran—to follow him. He told Martha that Mohammed was so strong and mighty that one day he decided to split the moon in half with his sword.

"Therefore," Hussein said, "once a month, we have the new moon come out in the sky."

Martha listened to Hussein patiently, smiled, and never said a word. Meanwhile, Martha preferred to pour her own tea rather than having Hussein serve her. Thus, she would often go into the kitchen and help herself to tea from the samovar. Once, as she was in the kitchen helping herself to a cup of tea, she asked Hussein if she could offer him some tea as well. Hussein protested, "No, madam. Pouring tea for the employees is my job. I am the one who is the servant around here, and not you."

Martha shook her head. "Hussein, for me, there are no servants and no masters. We're all equal."

Hussein smiled and said, "I know that you Armenians are Christian, but I don't know much about what your religion teaches. Can you enlighten me a bit?"

"Well," Martha answered, "Jesus's main teaching was for us to love one another sincerely. He even taught us to love our enemies."

"That's interesting, but tell me—how can you love your enemies?"

Martha responded, "Very simple. Just don't allow hatred in your heart. Besides, if we love everybody, we won't have any enemies. Don't you think so?"

Hussein began to walk out of the kitchen, but before leaving, he turned around, looked Martha in the eyes, and nodded his head approvingly. He said, "I like the idea of loving one another, but I still can't understand how we can love our enemies."

Martha sighed, "I know. It's not that simple, is it?"

Back at the funeral service, Martha drifted to Zaven's side for the last time, feeling quite heavy hearted. She hugged and kissed him and said farewell. She suddenly had to hold her breath. To her great disappointment, Martha noticed Zaven wearing his horrible pair of yellow boots that she vehemently hated, the same boots that she tried to get rid of a few times, to no avail. Martha even once left them at the garbage room for the maintenance workers at their Manhattan apartment building to throw away. Oh, how she was overjoyed! However, that same evening, when Zaven and Martha went for a walk on Broadway, they noticed a peddler selling the boots on the sidewalk. To her great chagrin, Zaven bought them back happily for five dollars.

Thus, when Martha noticed Zaven wearing her hated booths, she slapped her dear husband hard on the shoulder and laughed. Next, shaking a finger at him, Martha exclaimed, "How dare you, when you know how badly I hate these boots!"

Then, as Martha began stepping away toward the altar, she smiled mischievously and murmured to herself, "I guess now that I'll be gone from his life for good, he'll seriously need his beloved boots!"

Chapter 11

A New Dimension

Martha looked straight ahead, leaving her earthly life behind, and uttered, "Now I'm ready to start out. Let's leave before I change my mind."

"How can you change your mind? Your destiny is already set."

"I could wander over the earth forever, am I not correct?" she asked innocently.

"No, it doesn't work that way."

Martha heaved a sigh as she wore a crooked smile on her face. "Whatever. It's OK. Don't worry about me. I now feel better having talked about and remembered almost everything."

"Well," Sooren said, "I know we both can tell stories about our past lives until eternity, but I think you've gone through the most important memories, haven't you?"

"You bet I have. Let me now finish on a funny note, by adding that, although Zaven has lost his wife, at least I know he still has his precious yellow boots!" Martha joked, laughing her head off.

Sooren also laughed as Martha continued, "And dear Uncle, since I'm now pain-free, I can walk with you to the end of the earth."

Sooren arched his eyebrows as he grinned with satisfaction. "Is that so?" he asked. "Then, let's hurry up and push forward,"

"Do you think we could do one last thing before we take to the road?"

"What now?" Uncle Sooren said, throwing his hands up in the air.

"Do you think we could first visit Armen and his wife, Rosa, in Stuttgart, Germany, and then to Lily and her husband in Pasadena, California, before our final departure?"

"Why? Do you miss them?" Sooren asked with a broad smile.

"Of course I do. What a question," Martha answered, arching her eyebrows.

"I'm sorry. We can't, but don't worry. Your beloved sister and brother will join you in a few years, anyway."

Chapter 12

Free as a Bird

Within seconds, Martha found herself out in the open, zooming through thick clouds. At first, she felt unstable as she wobbled along, trying to follow her uncle. It was not easy; she had never flown like a bird. Martha found it hard to keep her balance. Nevertheless, she had no choice. Martha had to set her mind on flying; otherwise, she would drop like a dry swirling leaf right back down to the ground hundreds of miles below and have no more access to Sooren. Fortunately, she quickly learned to float. To her, it felt like being a wingless bird. Martha loved it, although it was scary as well as exhilarating.

Having left the clouds behind while soaring high through clear skies, Martha was enchanted by the sight of the multitude of tiny people scurrying like ants. Speeding vehicles down below looked like Matchbox cars.

"Oh, what a glorious feeling, dear Uncle. This is great!"

"I'm happy you are enjoying yourself. I promise you, there are many more interesting experiences awaiting you."

Martha took a deep breath of the fresh air as she now arrived shoulder to shoulder with her uncle. She rested a firm hand on his arm and began singing with pleasure. Sooren turned his head toward Martha and gave her a warm and satisfying grin.

As soon as Sooren discovered that Martha was moving forward with more ease, he began traveling at a breakneck speed. Martha did her best to keep up with him. What surprised her was the fact that it took them only seconds to fly over all those countries and even continents. They crossed high above the Pacific, the Atlantic, the Alps, then Australia, New Zealand, Greenland, Africa, and myriad other interesting spots on earth.

Now they were soaring like eagles above a vast piece of land, barely visible beneath a thin layer of mist. In no time, the voyage acquired a different realm of dimension. Martha felt like she was entering a zone and space with a unique type of pressure and atmosphere. Their travels reached such heights that Martha felt like she was sailing through space powered by solar winds.

"I love it! I love it!" she yelled joyously. "This is so much fun!" She beamed with satisfaction and thought, *I have already forgotten the feeling of life on earth. Oh, what a sensation! I had no idea it would be this much fun.*

In midair, Martha suddenly noticed two other spirit flyers hurtling alongside her and her uncle through the sky.

"Hey, Uncle Sooren, look at those two women flying by us. I wonder who they are."

Sooren turned around and beheld the two spirits floating at the same speed as they were. "I have no idea who they are."

Martha squinted to see clearly, as the two speeding women flying nearby inched closer. One of the flyers was a tall elderly woman with blond hair, blue eyes, and fair complexion. She was accompanying another woman who, like Martha, had recently died. The guide gazed at Martha and waved, while Martha waved back, examining her closely. The woman looked somewhat familiar to her. Then, all of a sudden, the woman shrieked, "Oh, my word! It's you, Martha. I had no idea you had died."

It did not take Martha long to recognize the person flying close by her as she yelled back, "My dear friend, Madeleine, I had no idea it was you traveling alongside us! What are you doing here?"

Madeleine responded, "I have come back to accompany my cousin to Heaven. By the way, let's meet once we arrive home."

"Yes, yes, let's do that!" Martha agreed as she and Sooren changed direction. Soon, she noticed more travelers in the air—some headed in the direction of Earth and others onward to Heaven.

Sooren asked Martha, "Tell me—who is this Madeleine character? I must say, she is very attractive."

"Oh, sorry, I should have introduced her to you. You are right; she is very good-looking. Madeleine was a friend of mine who died two years earlier. We used to play tennis together for years."

Sooren said, "It is so interesting that, like me, she has a mission to help a new spirit travel to her resting place."

"Yes, very interesting. By the way, Uncle, Madeleine used to be a model as a young woman. She also appeared on a TV show when she was younger."

Chapter 13

Planet Heaven

They entered a narrow and exceptionally long tunnel. Once inside, their flight took on a dizzying pace. As the air swished and buzzed in her ears and brushed against her skin, Martha perceived a brilliant light at the end of the tunnel thousands of miles away. For some reason, the trip through the mysterious passageway felt longer than the rest of their journey. After a while, they suddenly were beamed up—just like the crew on *Star Trek*—through a brilliantly lit gate into a luscious green meadow.

The uncle and niece took deep breaths, enjoying the aromatic, fresh pasture air as they sprawled on their backs, captivated by the sight of the crystalline sky. To Martha, it resembled a vast, high, bright diamond-studded ceiling. Within seconds, the air resounded with a soul-caressing melody. Martha listened with great interest. The tune somewhat resembled Bizet's compositions. When at the end of the song the broadcaster's voice echoed in the air, announcing that the musical piece was Gounod's work, Martha creased her brow, "I don't understand," she said. "Has Gounod changed his style?"

As Martha was busy pondering the composition of music, Uncle Sooren turned to Martha, gave her a lopsided smile, and said, "Welcome to Planet Heaven!"

Martha cocked her head and asked, "Excuse me? Did you say, 'Planet Heaven'? Already?"

He nodded.

"OK, but what do you mean by the word *planet*?"

"Well, on Earth, no one knows that Heaven is the same kind of a place as Earth—a separate planet."

"Go on; please fill me in," Martha said, creasing her brow pensively.

Sooren went on to explain that just like Earth, Heaven was divided into several continents.

Martha gazed into the luminous sky, which suddenly was swamped by numerous flocks of strange radiant fowl. Soon, the heavenly birds began flapping their broad wings to the rhythm of the ongoing classical melody.

"Listen, Uncle. I think this composition is Mozart's work. And the previous small piece we heard after Gounod's work was from Beethoven."

Sooren said approvingly, "I love classical music."

"So do I." Martha nodded in agreement as she scanned the surroundings. She wished to capture the beauty of the exceptional landscape in her memory. Martha had never seen such a stunning view. At the same time, a group of young women appeared not too far from the calm pond, meandering among the tall grass. The girls wore jeans and colorful sweaters as they bent down and picked flowers. The entire scenery looked like a fairyland.

Farther away, Martha noticed some teenagers enjoying themselves as they played soccer. She had to laugh at the sight of a few young men speeding on their motorcycles along the road, just like people did on Earth. However, she could not see any cars or carriages on the thoroughfare. She was interested to know what the official means of transportation were. Martha guessed that the motorcycle riders were there simply to enjoy themselves.

Chapter 14

The Great Reunion

The thought of meeting her father lit up Martha's heart. Gregor had been a mystery figure all through her long life. Anybody else who had lost a father at age eight and a half would have felt the same way. Naturally, she did not have the opportunity of getting to know him well. So, Martha was really looking forward to catching up on all those years he had not been around.

She could not wait to see her deceased mother, Anoosh, and two brothers, Arek and Artash, who had passed away a few years back as well. Martha thought they were special people. The same was true of her sister, Lily, and her brother Armen, both of whom were still living. They all were the kind of people who were serious one minute, and funny and easygoing the next.

Contrary to other severe and old-fashioned parents of those days, Anoosh was a modern and liberal-minded person who encouraged a pleasant atmosphere in their household. What's more, Anoosh respected her children and was always open to listen to their ideas. She treated them as friends and was ready to laugh and party with them. Her five children indeed felt lucky for having a mother such as her.

Martha, who herself had often been a fun mother and grandmother, was delighted to know that she soon would be meeting with her mother and brothers, as well as being in the company of all her other beloved departed ones, relatives and all. Yes, they all would be present at the welcoming party to greet her. Martha wondered if she could remember them all. It would be very embarrassing if a relative approached her and she did not remember who she or he was. It certainly would be interesting to see hundreds of aunts, uncles, cousins, and second cousins, some of whom she had never met when she was alive. Plus, her grandparents from both sides all had died many years before her birth. Martha was delighted to think that she would be uniting with so many relatives.

Chapter 15

The Same as on Planet Earth

As they marched forward, Martha kept narrating her life stories, and Sooren listened to them patiently. He had no choice. Sooren knew how all those incidents had marked his niece's life during her days on Earth. That's why she recounted them with such great enthusiasm. In the meantime, Sooren, trying to divert Martha's attention from her past, began talking about life in Heaven. He reminded Martha that Planet Heaven was not so much different from Earth, which had seven continents: Asia, Africa, North America, South America, Antarctica, Europe, and Australia. After their deaths, people automatically inhabited the same continent on Planet Heaven where they had lived on Earth. Nonetheless, they could change continents and countries depending on their own wishes.

Uncle Sooren told Martha that almost all of her kin lived in Iran on Planet Heaven. Martha thought that she had no difficulty living there, as she was born in that country and loved it tremendously. On the other hand, she knew for sure that Zaven would not be happy to live in Iran after his death. He had never liked Iran. In fact, the first thing he told Martha the day he met her, when they danced together after the American party at the Lucullus Night Club in Tehran, was, "I want to live abroad. I don't like Iran at all, and I would like you to come along with me."

Martha was flabbergasted to hear a stranger make such a bold suggestion. It had hardly been three hours since they had met. In the Armenian culture, boys were much more discreet and shyer than Zaven, who came across as being so aggressive.

Martha, turning to her uncle, said, "So, for the moment, I'll live in Iran, until Zaven arrives, and we decide where to establish ourselves."

"That makes sense."

"But Uncle, before all that, I have a mission to accomplish."

"Yes?" he asked. "What kind of a mission?"

Martha smiled pleasantly. "I need to find the famous musician Georges Bizet."

"What on Planet Heaven for?" Sooren joked.

"It's a long story. I'll tell you at the right time."

"OK. For the moment, let's concentrate on our journey to Iran," Uncle Sooren reminded her as he took out his iPhone from his pocket and punched something on it. Then he looked behind him and said, "Our destination is toward that direction."

Martha smiled. "It is interesting. Nothing has changed. Spirits rely on their iPhones the same way as people do on Earth!"

Chapter 16

Tehran on Planet Heaven

Sooren urged Martha to hurry. "We need to get to Tehran on time to attend the party."

"I'm ready, Uncle. Please lead the way, and I'll follow you happily."

At that point, Martha's uncle examined his iPhone for a second time and concluded that they should be heading westward toward Iran on Planet Heaven. Seeing that Sooren relied so much on his iPhone, Martha suddenly felt like having one, herself. However, she knew that when the right time came, she too could get an iPhone.

It was seven in the evening, and they were scheduled to arrive at the party in Tehran within the hour. The festivities began at eight. All they had to do after meeting the immediate family was to take showers and freshen up. Actually, Martha really wanted to change into a nicer outfit. She was sure that her mother would have a party dress to lend her. At present, she was dressed in black pair of pants and a red sweater, which was quite becoming.

As they began their trajectory, Martha asked, "Does each country in the seven continents have its special ruler?"

"No," Sooren answered. "There are no rulers on Planet Heaven, but God Himself manages Planet Heaven in its entirety."

"And the earth, too."

"Yes, indeed."

They arrived in exciting and colorful Tehran, where the streets bustled with life. It resembled the Tehran on Earth, except that as people rushed home after work, the cars flew a few feet from the ground. Martha noticed that the heavenly Iranians, exactly like the people in Tehran on Earth, were jaywalking through the crowded streets. Even like the actual Tehran, cars sometimes entered one-way streets in the opposite direction. Luckily, those streets were not usually busy ones.

On the sidewalks, clusters of young boys and girls happily chattered away. Above the shops, blinking lights advertised each store's goods and invited customers in. Contrary to the earthly Iranians, the women were not wearing headgear or chadors. Martha remembered how beautiful Iranian women always were. That was the same on Planet Heaven.

The evening air was nice and cool, filled with the aroma of special white, heavenly flowers blooming on green bushes all along the sidewalks. In the earthly Tehran, at nighttime in the summer, the scent of jasmine flowers saturated the pleasant evening air. Martha loved the aroma of the heavenly flowers. She took a deep breath and closed her eyes, smiling pleasantly. The whole atmosphere reminded her of her youth back in Tehran.

Martha looked at Sooren sheepishly as she said, "You know what, Uncle? Everything is so pleasant and beautiful.

The only thing which is missing for me is Zaven and my children!"

Martha's eyes welled with tears again. Uncle Sooren looked at her with sympathy and gave her a comforting pat on the shoulder.

Chapter 17

The Famous Avenue Kakh

Martha began to tremble with excitement. They were now strolling along Avenue Kakh, the same street where the Shah's majestic palace was located in the old days. In reality, the word *Kakh* in Farsi means "palace." As a teenager and later as a twenty-year-old woman, Martha lived on Avenue Kakh. As she walked down Avenue Kakh on Planet Heaven, Martha wondered if her family lived in the same house as on Earth. She did not ask her uncle about it. She wished for it to be a surprise.

Their earthly house used to be on two levels, with a small front yard located on the first floor. During summer evenings, Martha would sit on the veranda and read English novels to pass the time. Aside from reading books, Martha would busy herself with shopping and cooking for her family. This also relieved her mother a bit from her day-to-day chores. Martha would also translate books from English into

Farsi. The first book she translated was Martin Luther's story of life, especially written with children in mind. The publisher was impressed by the work of the eighteen-year-old Martha, whose Farsi was perfect. She wrote like an experienced writer, especially considering that her mother tongue was Armenian.

Years later, when Martha got married and gave birth to Sylvia, she would often visit her mother, brothers, and sister at their house on Avenue Kakh. One early afternoon, as she was strolling leisurely down that street with Sylvia, she was startled by the screeching sound of a car's tires. Martha turned her head to find a yellow Ferrari pulling over by their side. A man with a broad smile stared at Sylvia and her from behind the wheel. Martha thought the driver's face was familiar. Then, when she gave it some thought, she suddenly figured out that it was nobody else but the Shah himself. Martha bent down and asked Sylvia to wave at the Iranian monarch, and Martha, in turn, bowed her head to him respectfully. Then, as soon as Sylvia waved, the Ferrari zoomed away like a flying saucer.

Now, on Planet Heaven, Avenue Kakh looked as attractive to Martha as it did on Earth during her youth. Martha had been living on Avenue Kakh on Earth when she'd attended the American party where she'd met Zaven.

Chapter 18

Thinking of Mother on the Night of the American Party on Earth

The two travelers strolled down Avenue Kakh on Planet Heaven with smiling faces. Oh, that lovely, shady Avenue Kakh with its tall, majestic spruces and oaks lining its sidewalks. The charm of the street was further enhanced by some luxurious designer-clothing stores, stylish hair salons, and a large bakery filled with scrumptious Persian pastries, cakes, and sweets. And how about the street's bookstore, flower shops, and cinema? Martha became terribly nostalgic thinking of her past on Avenue Kakh. She saw herself as a young girl, going through a pleasant life with her loving family, especially that exceptional mother of hers. Naturally, Avenue Kakh also made Martha think of the day when she met Zaven…

During the party on Earth that night, Martha had sat idly on the sofa in the drawing room with her two friends,

Helen, a pretty Armenian girl, and Vahik, Martha's date. Martha blamed herself for not having stayed with her beloved mother. Instead of having fun, Martha was bored to death and tired of watching a multitude of strangers roaming around and enjoying themselves while drinking, eating, and dancing. Martha had told herself that if she had stayed with her mother, she would have had a better time.

True, that night she met Zaven, who was there with his American girlfriend. Sitting on the sofa daydreaming about her mother, Martha was totally unaware that destiny had brought her together with her future husband.

Almost every night at dusk in the summertime, Martha and her mother shared some happy moments together. After supper, when the weather turned completely dark and the moon reigned over the azure Tehran sky, they used to take their mattresses and covers out of the small rooftop storage room. Arranging them on individual little Persian carpets on the flat roof, with a clay pitcher of water next to them, they prepared to sleep outdoors in the cool weather. They lay on their bedding on the cool rooftop and drank cold, sour cherry syrup.

They would glue their eyes at the mesmerizing star-studded heavens, where the celestial torches seemed to be hanging far out above their heads. As they stared at the shiny sky for a while, it gave them the illusion of the stars being at arm's length. Martha, who had lived in several countries around the world, believed that the Tehran sky was prettier at night than anywhere else in the world. Yes, that same sky which was ablaze with millions of shiny stars and the bright moon.

Thinking about her mother on the night of the American party brightened Martha's mood a bit. She envisioned Anoosh's fair face, kind eyes, and shy smile. The young Martha's heart exploded with pleasure as her love for Anoosh flooded her whole being. Martha imagined her mother lying down on her bedding all by herself, thinking about God knows what…possibly her luxurious past life, or even her moody, unpredictable youngest daughter, Martha. Oh, how Martha missed her at that moment!

Martha both admired and respected Anoosh. To her, Anoosh was the epitome of a faultless mother. Everything she did seemed perfect to Martha. Anoosh was educated, intelligent, interesting, and self-sacrificing.

In those days, after Martha's father's death, Anoosh never bought anything new for herself. She always put her children first. Anoosh once said, "I have lived a luxurious life, both as a child and as a married woman."

"What do you mean?" Martha had asked.

"I mean, instead of my buying a new dress, my children should be the ones getting new stuff."

This would normally happen when they would be out together at a store, where they would see a beautiful dress. Martha or Lily would insist that their mother should buy that dress.

Since Martha was so good in the Farsi language and spoke it like a real Iranian, she helped her mother to pronounce the Persian words properly. Anoosh, like most Armenians, had a special accent. She had her education at Hubbard American School in the ancient city of Hamadan, where she was born. Although they studied Farsi once a week, their main languages of study were English and Armenian.

Martha laughed each time she remembered how her mother had learned Farsi at school. Their Farsi teacher was a mullah whom the girls never saw. He sat behind a curtain drawn on the platform in the classroom and taught the girls. In Iran during Anoosh's time, Muslims were very strict concerning male and female relationships. Naturally, schools were segregated. Men teachers were not allowed to stand in front of a classroom and teach girl students. Therefore, teachers in the American School were all women. They were either American missionaries or Armenians. In general, Persian girls did not get a chance to receive higher education in order to become teachers and so forth…Their parents forced them to marry as teenagers.

Anoosh's headmistress tried to abide by Islamic customs out of respect and protected the students from being seen by or having contact with strange men.

The mullah, teaching Farsi to the girls from behind the curtain, knew them only by the tone of their voices and their names. Anoosh, being the naughtiest girl in her class, gave him a hard time. She giggled and sneered in order to make the students laugh as the mullah went on teaching. Anoosh related to Martha that the mullah kept calling out, "Anoosh… Anoosh, please be quiet!" It was obvious that Anoosh had no interest in Farsi lessons in those days. As an adult, she considered her daughter to be her real teacher.

What Martha liked the most about her mother was her ability to be friends with her children. Indeed, she was Martha's best friend. Martha felt free to talk about any subject with her mother. Moreover, Anoosh had no problem with her children criticizing her. Something else that Anoosh's children liked about their mother was that they could tease her and even give her comic Persian and Armenian nicknames. All she did was to giggle and make them laugh with her contagious hilarity.

In fact, every single member of the family loved to frolic and laugh together, even during the days of hardship after Martha's father's death.

Another thing Martha appreciated about her mother was her wisdom and philosophy about life. She was humble and profound. Martha could never forget what Anoosh told her once.

In the days when Martha, Zaven, and the children lived in France, Anoosh also lived with them and used to help Martha around the house. Late one night, when everybody else was in bed, Martha found her mother polishing up the kitchen. Martha told her that she should not work at such a late hour. She stressed that Anoosh should be in bed. Anoosh had laughed and said, "Oh, my dear, don't worry about me not sleeping."

"I do worry," Martha said. "Mama, you should try to get a good night's rest."

Anoosh responded, "My dear, soon, there'll be no end to how much I'll sleep and rest. Yes, as the saying goes, I'll take the great rest, or better to say, the great sleep." She then smiled lovingly and added, "So, my lovely daughter, let me work while I'm still *awake*."

Martha, now residing on Planet Heaven and thinking about her mother's wise words, told herself that Anoosh was definitely correct. Everybody without exception takes the great rest when the right time comes. In fact, Martha mused, wasn't she presently relishing the everlasting repose? The same relaxed and pain-free state of the so-called great sleep?

When Anoosh uttered those words, Martha thought of the famous twelfth-century Persian poet, Omar Khayyam's words, "Arise, we have eternity for sleeping!"

Chapter 19

Welcome Home

Martha and her uncle stood behind the same blue wooden door where Martha had lived in Tehran as a young girl. She took a deep breath as she rang the doorbell with a trembling finger and a thumping heart. Martha could not believe that she was about to climb the long and curvy staircase that she used to dash up as a young girl more than ten times a day, sixty years earlier. As Martha stood there, overcome by anticipation, her mind kept churning with questions. Meanwhile, she was extremely excited at the thought of soon visiting her family members. Luckily, she did not have to wait long. Within seconds, a head stuck out through the small window on the top floor.

"Oh my God!" a voice resonated down from above. "Thank God, you two are finally here!"

Upon hearing the familiar voice, Martha said happily, "Hooray! It's Artash, Uncle Sooren!"

Martha loved her eldest brother dearly. Despite having a reputation for being bad tempered, Artash always had been nice to his youngest sister when he was alive. In fact, he had spoiled Martha immensely and showered her with unconditional love, probably because Martha did not take his edginess and anger seriously. What's more, she made him laugh a lot with her clownish behavior. As a young girl, she was very humorous and loved to make people laugh. In that respect, Martha tremendously resembled her mother.

As the thumping sound of her brother's footsteps descending the long staircase filled the air, Martha hardly could wait to get inside the house. She felt extremely excited and overjoyed at the thought of seeing Artash, who had passed away ten years earlier.

Finally, when her eldest brother opened the door and hugged his newly arrived sister, Martha noticed that he looked younger and in much better shape than he had appeared on Earth during the last few years of his life.

Arthash led the way as they mounted the stairs. Before reaching the last step on the second landing, Martha heard muffled laughter, chatter, and music. She realized that they must be a bit late and that the party must have begun. This meant they could not take showers and freshen up.

When the door to the apartment opened, the guests suddenly ceased talking and faced the entrance where Martha, Artash, and Uncle Sooren stood. Martha scanned the faces one by one. There were approximately twenty people present. A long, rectangular table was placed at the center of the room, spread with different kinds of colorful salads, beans, peas, vegetables, and rice dishes. Martha did not perceive any serving dishes containing meat. *Of course*, she thought. *This is Heaven. Animals are left alone. Exactly my kind of a place.* Being an animal lover, she didn't like to eat meat when she was alive.

Each time that she had to eat chicken or any type of seafood, she felt guilty. She especially never ate lobster because of the way they were thrown alive in boiling water to cook.

As she stood there, frozen like a statue, not knowing how to act, a well-dressed middle-aged man—balding but tall, slim, and pleasant looking—stepped forward and embraced her.

"I can't believe you are the same person who used to be my eight-year-old little girl back on Earth, whom I left seventy years ago," he said as his eyes welled with tears.

"Oh, Father, it's you. It's you! You can't imagine how much I've wished to see you from the moment I've set foot onto Planet Heaven!"

Her father, Gregor, wiped his tears and hugged her again.

Martha found it strange for Gregor to look so much younger than she and uttered, "Funny, isn't it, that your eight-year-old girl should now look older than you, right?"

He beamed lovingly and did not answer.

Soon, Anoosh, her mother rushed forward and kissed Martha. She was wearing a black-and-white polka-dot dress, and her face looked young, with sparkling eyes and glistening silver hair. Arek, her other brother, who had recently left Earth, followed. Presently, their relatives encircled her. Martha mostly recognized them. She saw none of her grandparents or great-grandparents.

After the greeting rituals were over, she found herself staring hard at Gregor. Having lost him when she was so young, she did not really know anything about a father-daughter relationship. So it was hard for Martha to tell how she felt about Gregor. In fact, Martha was not at all sure what kind of person he really was.

How could I know him well anyway, she thought, *having been separated from him for over half a century?*

The only way Martha thought she could bond with her father was to try to transport herself to the days of her childhood, when Gregor was still living. Martha tried hard to remember her father back in the days when she was seven or eight. If she could achieve bringing the past back, Martha thought, then she might be able to establish an emotional tie with him.

Luckily, her endeavors were fruitful. Martha could more or less relate with her past feelings toward her father, and with the passage of every second, she commenced to establish some real feelings about Gregor. What helped her the most to achieve this state of mind were the memories of their trips to the ancient city of Hamadan. Gregor had been born and raised in Hamadan, although he and his family lived in the city of Arak. However, since all his relatives lived in Hamadan, Gregor made a point to take his wife and children to his hometown regularly for the summer holidays. He wished for their children to know who they really were by mingling with their uncles, aunts, and cousins. In Arak, they were quite isolated.

Martha's first memory of a trip to Hamadan with her father was when she was seven years old. They stayed in Hamadan for one month and then returned to their beautiful, mansion-type home in Arak. Arak was and still is a strict Islamic city in Iran, where Martha and her four siblings were born. Martha and her family lived there only until she was eleven years old, when they moved to Tehran.

Their relatives in Hamadan lived in a district within the city called Sar-Ghaleh. *Sar-Ghaleh* in Farsi means "the fortress on top of the hill." That specific area was an Armenian enclave in those days. Nowadays, however, all the Armenians have moved mostly to the United States and Europe. The only reminders of Armenian heritage still existing in Hamadan are the derelict Armenian Gregorian and Presbyterian churches.

Martha never thought that she would feel certain emotions on Planet Heaven, but when she remembered her uncle's words about everything regarding Planet Heaven being the replica of Earth, she realized that she, as a human being, was exactly the same person as she used to be on Earth. Therefore, there was a reason for her feelings regarding her relationship with Gregor.

Chapter 20

Gisak

While conversing with her loving family members and relatives, Martha noticed her uncle staring at her pensively. He smiled and began advancing toward her, Martha arched an eyebrow. "What's up?" she asked Sooren when he reached her.

"I can't stop wondering why you want to look for Georges Bizet. Something doesn't seem to be right."

"No," Martha answered. "Nothing's wrong. Georges Bizet is one of my favorite composers. I especially love his opera *Carmen*."

"Is that so?" Sooren asked skeptically.

"Yes, Uncle. I promise you. Besides, his unfortunate life story has always made me think of my own occasional disappointments in life."

They had to stop their conversation when a white-complexioned man with blue eyes, steel-rimmed glasses, and light-brown thinning hair approached them. Martha gazed at him and tried hard to remember who he was. His face was familiar. The man moved forward and said, "Hi, Martha. You don't seem to remember me, do you?"

Martha creased her brow pensively. *Dear Lord, who can he be?* she mused. She was sure that he was kin, because he resembled somebody in the family—but who? Martha concentrated hard and tried to travel into the past. Then, suddenly, it came to her. "Yes, of course!" she exclaimed. "How could I not recognize you right away, dear Gisak!"

"Well, I'm not surprised. How could you remember me? You were only a girl of eleven when I left Tehran for the United States." He grinned, shook his head, and added, "If I didn't know who the guest of honor was today, and if I had bumped into you accidentally, I, too, would not have recognized who you were, Martha. So, don't feel embarrassed at all."

Martha embraced her cousin fondly and said, "I will never forget how you saved me when I was an eleven-year-old girl."

Her cousin nodded in agreement. "Yes. I also remember that day vividly. I can't imagine what could have happened to you if you had stayed out in the street all night by yourself."

Gisak happened to be one of Martha's favorite cousins.

He was fifteen years her senior. He was the son of Martha's father's middle brother, Norman. She had such fond memories of him, which made her smile with love and pleasure.

The event Martha and Gisak began talking about that night happened soon after Martha's family had moved to Tehran. Gisak recently had graduated from medical school at the time. Martha had been very proud to know that she had a cousin who was a doctor.

When they first arrived in Tehran, Martha used to go to school with her older brother, Arek. They took a long ride to school by bus early in the morning and returned home about five or six in the evening.

In the morning, after arriving at the crossroads of Naderi Avenue and Ghavam Saltaneh Street, Martha walked south toward Mehr American Elementary School. Arek proceeded north to his high school. Around four thirty, when school was over, sister and brother met at the same location where they had parted in the morning. From there, they walked about half a mile to the bus station to go home.

Martha counted on Arek to lead the way. She had no idea where to get on and off the bus in order to go home. Even if she did know at which station to get off, she wouldn't know which way to walk the few blocks to get home.

One afternoon, Martha arrived at their usual meeting place, but her brother was not there. Normally, he always arrived before Martha. She became apprehensive. *Where is he?* she wondered. Martha thought she had no choice but to wait until he showed up. Unfortunately, little did she know what was in store for her. Martha waited and waited. An hour passed, and Arek was still absent.

Oh, dear God, what am I supposed to do? I can't stay all by myself out in the street! Where will I sleep tonight? Martha panicked. To make things worse, she needed to use the bathroom badly.

Martha walked back and forth along the block on Naderi Avenue and began to cry. Meanwhile, pedestrians rushed past her, without paying any attention to a devastated little girl. The sun began to set. There were no children seen on that busy, crowded sidewalk, nor any women. The streetlights began to come on, and the lamps above the storefronts already had begun to blink and flash.

That's it! I have no choice but to search for a hidden corner or alley where I can lie down and sleep, she told herself. She thought she would freeze sleeping without any covers all night outdoors. This was November, and the weather was quite cold.

Right when little Martha was about to head back to Ghavam Saltaneh Street, she spotted a familiar face approaching through the dense crowd. The fellow was carrying a doctor's bag in his hand and wore thin, steel-rimmed glasses. As he drew closer, his familiar blue eyes opened wide with surprise upon noticing Martha all by herself. He immediately quickened his steps as he rushed toward her and hugged her hard. "Hey, Martha, what are you doing all by yourself among this busy crowd?"

Thank you, God. It was her guardian angel, Gisak, who had come to save Martha from her devastating fate. Martha clung to Gisad and asked, crying, "Please, Gisak, can you take me home? I'm so scared!"

Gisak smiled, bobbing his head. Then, holding Martha's hand, he led her to the bus to take her home.

That was the kind of cousin Gisak was—caring, kind, and loving. Not only did Gisak save her that day from an upsetting situation, but each time that she got sick as a child, he would show up at their doorstep, carrying his impressive, shiny black-leather medical case.

The day Gisak saved Martha on Naderi Avenue, Arek looked extremely distressed when he came home later that evening. He told his family members that the teacher had kept them in class for two extra hours. No matter how much Arek begged the teacher to make an exception in his case and let him go, he refused. When Arek had explained why he insisted on leaving at exactly four o'clock, the teacher had reassured him that his sister would be all right.

Chapter 21

A Pleasant Surprise at the Party on Planet Heaven

Sooren nudged Martha, "Hey, we didn't finish our conversation about your reasons for looking for the French composer. We were interrupted by your cousin."

"Yes, we were. But, what else do you want to know? I've told you everything"

"I want to understand once you find Bizet, what are you going to do with him? Really, what plans do you have?"

Martha had hardly begun explaining, when she sensed a gentle pat on her shoulder. Feeling tired of speaking with her relatives, she completely ignored it. As she prepared to answer her uncle, she felt another tap on her shoulder. Martha turned around reluctantly, and suddenly burst out, "What?"

Martha covered her mouth with the palm of her hand as her jaw dropped. She felt mystified and flabbergasted. "Oh dear. Oh dear! Marie, I never believed that I could ever have the opportunity to see you in Iran on Planet Heaven. My dear friend, how on earth did you figure out where to find me?"

Martha shook her head and began laughing like mad, as her heart pounded loudly with joy. "No, really, is this possible?" she asked fervently, hugging her beloved friend against her chest.

Marie smiled amiably and did not answer. As always, she appeared calm and collected. She stood graciously, with her hands folded in front of her, and glued her eyes at Martha. Anoosh, meanwhile, rushed to their side and wrapped an arm around Marie's shoulder and said, "Marie traveled all the way from America to surprise you."

"Oh, Marie, let me introduce you to my uncle, Sooren," Martha said, as she placed her hand against Sooren's back and pushed him forward toward Marie.

"Glad to meet you," Sooren said politely as he bowed in front of Marie and shook her hand.

In the meantime, Martha shook her head, feeling astounded. She still could not believe that her beloved friend would travel to Iran from the United States when she learned that Martha was on her way to Planet Heaven.

Chapter 22

The Four Musketeers

Marie had been a wonderful friend before she died a few years earlier. Right before her death, Zaven and Martha had moved to Abu Dhabi, where they had lived for a year and a half because Zaven was transferred to the United Arab Emirates on business.

Marie was the same friend who played tennis with Martha, Michele, and Marcia on Fridays at the health club–where they were known as the Four Musketeers.

Soon after Zaven and Martha moved to Abu Dhabi, Marie suddenly discovered that she had an advanced case of lung cancer. She had wanted to visit them, but being unable to travel, she asked Martha in an e-mail: "Please be my eyes in the UAE. Try to transport Abu Dhabi and Dubai to my living room in Riverhead."

Martha not only fulfilled her friend's wish by writing descriptive e-mails, she also regularly e-mailed her the chapters of her new book, which she had begun writing in Abu Dhabi. Then, exactly at the time when Martha's manuscript was completed, Marie's life reached its end. It was as if she had made a conscious decision to stay alive until she had read the complete manuscript. Marie's daughter, Ruth, had seen how the chapters from Martha's book and her e-mails had helped to ease Marie's suffering, so she had made her mother a solemn promise that she would print Martha's manuscript and bury it with her. Martha was happy to know Marie's illness had been more tolerable because of all her e-mails and the chapters from her book, *The Passionflower*. Martha also had been proud that she had been able to share Arab ways of life, the desert, the camels, and the ultramodern emirates of Abu Dhabi and Dubai not only to Marie's living room in Riverhead but to her bedroom as well when, toward the end of her life, she could no longer get out of bed.

Chapter 23

Back to the Party on Planet Heaven

At her parents' party on Planet Heaven, Martha gazed at Marie compassionately and said, "I had no idea how pleasant it would be to rejoin you, my good friend, and also my family members on Planet Heaven. And here I am, standing, talking with you, and everybody else."

Martha took a deep breath. "Now tell me, Marie, did you find my e-mails about Abu Dhabi, Dubai, and even Saudi Arabia interesting? In other words, did I do a good job of acting as your eyes?"

Martha had visited Saudi Arabia with Zaven for a week while they lived in Abu Dhabi.

"Yes, my dear," Marie responded. "You sure did! Not only did you become my eyes, but you stirred my curiosity so skillfully that I decided to travel to the United Arab Emirates on both planets after my death to see things with my own eyes."

"What did you think about the UAE on Earth?"

"It was exactly as you had described in your e-mails for me. I also liked the way you had depicted the people living in that land."

Martha rubbed her chin thoughtfully. "Marie, I am so curious to find out if women and men dress the same way on the Planet Heaven UAE as they do in UAE on Earth."

Marie shook her head, grinning broadly. "No, my dear friend, not at all."

"Not at all? You mean they dress like the Westerners on Planet Heaven?"

"That's exactly right!" Marie uttered. "We all know how dark-colored clothing make the summer heat feel much worse."

Martha answered dreamily, "It is good to know that on Planet Heaven, Arab women are free to dress and move about as they wish."

Martha, having a rebellious character ever since her youth, could never accept that men should be more privileged than women, the way she found it to be in certain countries. While Martha considered Arab women to be suppressed and under-privileged creatures compared to men, Arab women themselves seemed to be very content with their status within their society.

As a foreigner, Martha had no problem dressing the way the Saudi women did—in long robes—during her visit in that land. She accepted that foreign women as guests had to respect and abide by the Islamic laws concerning women's appearance and behavior in public. Yet in Western countries, nobody forced foreigners to abide by any specific European or American customs. If an Arab or other Muslim woman wished to wear her hijab, nobody forbade her from doing so. Yes, they were free.

As Marie looked at her friend thoughtfully, Martha remembered her trip to Saudi Arabia. She told Marie how, at the hotel, as she'd sat at the café one morning, hoping to have breakfast, the waiter approached her and barked, "You can't sit here. This area is reserved for men."

Thus, the waiter forced Martha out and pointed her toward the direction of a dark café located behind the men's designated eating area. Although she felt a bit belittled, Martha obeyed and moved to the gloomy café for women. Naturally, all the servers at the women's café were female. What had Martha been thinking when she'd sat in the men's café and expected to be served by a male waiter? Did she think she was in Europe or America? Male waiters waited on male guests in Saudi Arabia, not women. The only time they waited on women was if the women were accompanied by their husbands.

Martha carried on with her story about Saudi Arabia and the treatment of women in society. "I was really offended to be treated so despicably by an arrogant masculine waiter."

She went on to tell Marie the story of her and Zaven's dinner party in the palatial mansion of a prominent Saudi sheik.

Martha explained to Marie that the moment they had arrived, men and women were ushered to separate rooms. Of course, when the men were not around, the women did not have their headgear and abayas on. They all had nice hairdos and designer outfits. She added that having seen the women during the day wearing their Islamic outfits, she had difficulty recognizing them without their hijabs. Martha told Marie that during dinner, while making some small talk, the hostess had asked Martha if she liked Saudi Arabia. Martha had nodded. "Yes; it is very nice. The only thing that bothers me is the way women are treated here."

"What do you mean?" the hostess had asked, sounding offended.

Martha recounted her experience during breakfast time in the hotel restaurant and asked, "Why are women discriminated against? How can women accept not to be treated as equally as men in public?"

The hostess had smiled, taking a long drag from her cigarette, and retorted, "We women are very happy to be living under the shadow of men. They provide us with a comfortable living. Materially, we are extremely well taken care of. Yes, they are the bread earners, the heads of our families, and we respect them."

Another young, dark-complexioned woman, called Khadijah, cut in. "Besides, we women believe that the more we sacrifice ourselves on this earth, the better treatment we will earn in our afterlife existence."

Marie listened intently as Martha described the hostess stressing confidently, with her arched, thinly plucked eyebrows, "Khadijah, you should not use the word *sacrifice*. Instead, you should say, 'The more we humble ourselves, the better we will be rewarded in Heaven.'"

Marie said, "I wonder where they get such ideas from."

Martha answered, "I don't know! But don't we have certain Christians with the same kind of naïve beliefs?"

Marie nodded.

Martha continued, "Some such simple-minded people who take their religious leaders' fanatical teachings seriously can be really scary."

"Oh yes, like the ignorant terrorists who believe that by blowing themselves up, as well as all those innocent people, they will be rewarded for their sacrifice by the gift of forty virgins when they enter Heaven."

Martha giggled as she suddenly remembered a funny anecdote. "You know what, Marie? This reminds me of a joke that a friend had forwarded me in e-mail form some time ago."

Marie beamed and said, "I'm ready for a good laugh. Go ahead. Tell me the story."

Martha visualized the funny picture on her computer screen as she recounted the joke. "This is how the story goes: A terrorist who blew himself up at the marketplace, killing dozens of people, was waiting at Heaven's gate to enter. When he set foot through the gate, he found forty severe-looking virgin nuns in their long, black habits, with machine guns pointed at him."

Chapter 24

The Barman

Martha turned around and looked at the bar, where her father was busy serving drinks. She said, "Now, let's put the subject of Saudi, Abu Dhabi, and other UAE lands behind us."

"OK. I know what you're going to suggest we do instead."

"Oh yes? What?"

"You're going to rub the palms of your hands together and say, like you did on Earth, 'Let's have a drink!'"

"That's exactly what I was about to suggest. By the way, do you still like vodka tonic?"

"Yes, I still love it. The good news is that you can get all the different brands on Planet Heaven, including SKYY, our favorite vodka!"

Martha draped an arm around Marie and began to laugh.

"Why are you laughing?" Marie gazed at her friend, utterly surprised.

"I just thought that dying is not such a bad thing after all."

"Yeah. If only people on Earth knew about it!"

As Marie and Martha were busy giggling like teenagers, Uncle Sooren approached them and said, "Don't you want to move on, Martha? Haven't you gabbed enough?"

"I'm having such a great time, Uncle! I wish I could stay here forever!"

"Don't worry. We can always come back to your parents, whenever you wish, and party to your heart's desire. Now, let's get going."

Martha had forgotten how seriously Uncle Sooren always had taken his responsibilities in life. And now, he thought he had a mission to help his niece to find the famous French musician.

Marie, completely ignoring Sooren, turned to Martha and interjected, "One more story about the UAE and then I'll stop and let you leave with your uncle."

Martha laughed. "OK, one more, and then we'll seriously quit talking about it."

"Do you want to hear which of your e-mails amused me the most?"

"Tell me. Which one?" Martha smiled, looking eager to hear Marie's answer.

Marie looked at Sooren apologetically. He smiled at her and nodded. "Go ahead. One more story, and then it's going to be good-bye for now."

"I promise you that after this one, I'll shut up," she said. "I loved the story of you, Zaven, Sylvia, and little Leon having been stranded in the hot desert. It sounded so frightening!"

Sylvia and her son, the cuddly Leon, who was hardly two years old, visited Martha and Zaven in Abu Dhabi during the month of August. The weather was unbearably hot, probably somewhere around 120 degrees Fahrenheit. Obviously, it was not fun walking outside in the streets. So, they retreated to their freezing-cold apartment, where they had no control over the thermostat. It was set at a certain temperature, and no matter how badly Martha tried to change it, it would not work.

So, whenever Martha felt too cold, she simply stepped outside onto their long, curved terrace with glass banisters. Their luxurious thirty-seventh-floor apartment overlooked the turquoise waters of the Persian Gulf. It is so funny that the extreme heat on their terrace felt so pleasant to Martha, compared to the unbearable cold of their apartment.

One Friday, Zaven decided to drive to Ras al-Khaimah, approximately thirty miles away from Abu Dhabi, to show Sylvia the famous, tall dunes of the area. Unfortunately, they had no idea what was in store for them when they set off.

The dune area outside Ras al-Khaimah was totally deserted when they arrived there around noon. Zaven decided to pull into the parking lot at the foot of the lofty, impressive sandbanks, so they could have a close look at them without leaving the car. They were aware of the scorching heat of a desert land. Especially with a toddler, it could be very dangerous.

After having a good look at the gigantic range of dunes, Zaven tried to back out of the parking lot. However, because the whole parking area was sandy, the tires started turning in place without the car budging an inch. They were stuck, and it was worse than being caught in the snow. No matter how hard Zaven tried to move either forward or backward, the tires sank deeper and deeper into the sand. To make matters worse, the dune zone appeared to be deserted. Thus their chance of getting help seemed to be impossible. Probably nobody even considered visiting the area in the heat of August.

Chapter 25

Total Desperation

What were they supposed to do? How could they be protected from the blistering desert heat? The other problem was that they had to keep the car engine running to cool themselves, which meant they could run out of gas. That also would be disastrous. The only thing that could save them from that scary situation would be a real miracle. To make things worse, there was yet another big difficulty. Sylvia had brought along her two-year-old son. None of them wanted any harm to come to their darling little boy. They didn't even have any spare bottles of water. All they had was half a bottle of lukewarm water left among them. Zaven tried several times in vain to contact the local police on his cell phone for help, but there were no telephone connections in the desert. The situation was indeed terrifying.

Just when hope seemed lost, two young men staggered toward the car. They had on white Pakistani outfits, which included baggy pants with long tunics draped over them. As their pants flapped around in the sand, Martha and Sylvia felt somewhat relieved but also apprehensive. They wondered if these young men were friendly to non-Muslims.

As Martha was busy anticipating different scenarios in her head, the two young men walked straight to the car, without stopping to talk with Zaven. They opened the car door, and one of them said something in Arabic.

Martha told the fellow, "Sorry, we don't speak Arabic."

He turned toward his friend and looked at him quizzically. Then, the other young Pakistani said in broken English, "I speak English a little."

"Oh, thank God for that!" Sylvia exclaimed, not allowing her mother to answer.

Zaven, in the meantime, was wading from the opposite direction through the deep sand toward the car. The English-speaking young fellow looked at Martha and asked, "Are you American?"

Martha hesitated for a second. She was not sure whether it was wise for her to admit that they were US citizens, in case these men hated Americans. She said, "We were born in Iran."

"Oh, Iran! Nice. Please come out of the car. Yes, yes, come to our trailer. I will give you cold water and tea."

Sylvia murmured, "Mom, I wonder what would have happened if we had said we were US citizens."

Martha gave Sylvia a lopsided smile instead of an answer.

The two young men then led the women and the child to their mobile home, which was nice and cool. Two large fans hummed loudly inside. They all sat down on the floor, which was covered with small, poor-quality Persian rugs, as a third fellow appeared from behind a curtained door carrying a tray with three glasses of water and two cups of tea.

While the women and the toddler enjoyed their refreshments, two of the men helped Zaven drive the car out of the parking lot. They placed some planks of wood under the rear and front wheels and drove it out of the deep sand. Of course, Zaven tipped the two kind rescuers generously.

Chapter 26

The UAE Residents Inhabiting Both Planets

"Marrrthaaa!" Uncle Sooren called out with a funny voice from the other end of the room. This was the third time he was interrupting her warm conversation with Marie. Martha was beginning to think that without her, Sooren would be completely bored. She had never thought of asking him what his profession on Planet Heaven was before he took over the responsibility of helping her. She admitted that he had done a great job of helping her acclimate to the heavenly atmosphere. Nevertheless, now she wished to be a bit more independent, although she loved her uncle's company immensely.

Dragging Marie behind her, she walked toward Sooren, threw an arm around his shoulder, and uttered softly, "Please, Uncle! I know we have to start our search for Bizet. But an hour longer won't make a big difference in our plans."

Marie nodded, looking at Martha approvingly. She had traveled all that way to spend some quality time with her old buddy. In addition, although earlier they had decided to stop talking about the United Arab Emirates, it seemed that they were not done with their stories yet.

Even so, Martha suddenly realized that she had been a bit curt with her kind uncle. She threw an apologetic glance toward him and beamed bashfully. Fortunately, Sooren did not appear to be offended. He slumped into a comfortable armchair, smiling at them both. Martha took a sigh of relief and winked at him.

Turning her attention back to Marie, Martha said, "Marie, you have already told me about the way men and women dress in the UAE on Planet Heaven. Now tell me your opinion concerning the culture here on Planet Heaven, in comparison to those living on planet Earth."

Marie nodded. "I'm so glad you asked. Come to think of it, I really think that there is a big difference between the characteristics of those separate worlds on the two planets. As you had explained in your e-mails, the ones inhabiting the UAE on Earth came across as a bit unsociable, especially when it concerned their relationships with foreigners living on their land."

Marie sighed, shaking her head unapprovingly. "I felt so sad thinking of the poor foreign workers slaving in the scorching heat. I understand many of those workers die because of the inhumane conditions of life."

"Yes, they do. Unfortunately, they are not even well paid. And their living quarters in the UAE are horrendous," Martha said. "In general the UAE citizens don't like foreigners. Remember the story of the young woman with her lively two-year-old girl that I wrote to you about?"

"Which one do you mean?"

"The one I met that morning at La Brioche Café. She openly told me that she was not happy having all those foreigners living in her country."

While living in Abu Dhabi, Martha often used to go to La Brioche Café to enjoy a cup of cappuccino and a croissant. Unlike Saudi Arabia, in Abu Dhabi as well as in Dubai, public places were not segregated. Black-attired, hijab-wearing women mingled with people of both genders.

One morning at La Brioche, a two-year-old Abu Dhabi girl whose mother was sitting at the table next to Martha kept running to Martha and rambling about something to her in Arabic.

"Hi, sweet little girl. Unfortunately, I don't speak any Arabic and can't understand what you're saying," Martha said, looking apologetically at the small child and her mother.

The mother wore her black abaya with her head completely covered by her headgear. She said in perfect English, "I'm so sorry for my daughter bothering you." Then, suddenly, she stood and ran to catch the unruly and lively girl. She soon returned to her seat and continued talking with Martha, "Where are you from?"

"New York," Martha answered.

"Do you like living in Abu Dhabi?"

"Yes, it is very nice."

"Well, I personally don't like my country anymore," she said, shaking her head.

The woman told Martha that since the United Arab Emirates had been completely modernized, nothing felt the same anymore. She said that she remembered how she loved to walk barefoot on the sand as a young girl. She added that she also used to love the traditional huts and tents, contrary to all those Western-style high rises and plush villas. What she detested most of all, she said, was having foreigners living in her country.

She claimed that the foreign workers gaped at her teenage daughter with lustful eyes.

Martha told Marie that she thought the reason the workers gawked at young women was because they had no women of their own. They were not permitted to bring their wives with them. They could return to their countries to visit their families, but only for a month, after completing their two-year work contract in the UAE.

"Marie," Martha asked, "do the UAE residents on Planet Heaven like to mix with foreigners?"

"Oh, yes. First, as I said before, they are dressed as Westerners. Second, everybody mingles with everybody else. The atmosphere is totally international."

Chapter 27

Playing Tar on Planet Heaven

Before Martha had a chance to say good-bye to Marie, she suddenly heard somebody playing the Iranian guitar-like instrument called *tar*. She turned around to see who the tar player was, and discovered it was her dear father, Gregor. Before dying at the age of fifty, Gregor had met a fundamentalist sect of Christians, who had convinced him to become a born-again Christian. The conditions for Gregor joining this strict cult of Christianity were to stop smoking, drinking, and playing the tar. Gregor, who was a skillful tar player, agreed to accept all these conditions, so he gave away his tar to a close friend. Now in Heaven, it was all right for him to play tar, dance, and drink alcohol in moderation. Martha, who had been a fun-loving person all her life, even until her death in her late seventies, felt the same way on Planet Heaven. She was now surrounded by her loved ones and adored every second of it. It was obvious that she would continue being a fun-loving soul.

The day of her welcoming party, Martha was ecstatically happy with the pleasant atmosphere of her parents' home on Planet Heaven. Indeed, she was so joyful that she could not help clapping her hands to the rhythm of her father's tar playing.

Martha burst into the center of the room with the speed of a young girl and pulled Marie behind her. As the two friends began twisting and moving cheerily to the tune of Gregor's music, all the other guests also joined in to dance.

Soon, the room began to feel like a blaring disco. Martha's behavior brought about an incredible fun, party mood. Gregor continued playing even more, happier songs, which made the guests sing and clap their hands vigorously. For a second, Martha forgot that she was in paradise. Being merry was nothing new to her. She was born to have joy in her heart almost perpetually. Every time she and Zaven got the chance to join their loved ones for a special occasion, they would have nothing but great fun together. Now she was continuing to do this with the spirits.

A year before Martha died, Zaven organized a surprise birthday party for her in Manhattan at a Mexican restaurant called Cilantro. She was overjoyed to have all their family members with her. Their grandchildren had surrounded her and were constantly hugging and kissing her. She was de-lighted to see her darling granddaughter, Hilda, who worked every day until late hours into the night, present, along with the beloved Alain and Alenoosh. Although the next day was a school day, they had made a point to attend. The same was true with her precious grandson, Leon. Indeed, she felt blessed. They all showered her with excellent gifts, but to her, the best gift of the evening was the contents of a card written by her beautiful granddaughter Alenoosh. It read:

Dear Martha (her grandchildren called her by her first name),

Happy Birthday. I just wanted to let you know that you are the world's most wonderful Grandma. Whenever we spend time together, I feel like I'm talking to one of my best friends. I'm so happy that we have such a great relationship. I'm very thankful for it. You and Zaven are definitely two of my favorite people in our family, just because you're both so different and easy to talk to. I enjoy every moment that I spend with you, and I will never get tired of listening to your stories. You are the most beautiful, funny, and cool Grandma anyone could ask for, and I'm so thankful to have you in my life. Thanks for never feeling like an old lady! Ha, ha! You're awesome.

I love dancing with you.
Your granddaughter,
Alenoosh

Chapter 28

The Journey Begins

That night, on Planer Heaven, Martha looked at her father and smiled, thinking, *No wonder all my life, I acted the way I did on Earth, sometimes having a drink or two, dancing, and having fun. Not only do I cherish my fun mother, but I am also like my father.* Martha was so pleased at the chance to get to know the real Gregor on Planet Heaven. Now, she could catch up with all those lost years on Earth.

At that instant, Martha's father walked toward her and Marie carrying two vodka martinis.

"Here, girls. I know you both need to leave soon, so have a drink each for the road."

After saying good-bye to Marie and hugging her family members warmly, Martha and her uncle left the Avenue Kakh apartment. Their destination was to catch the fast-rolling escalator that operated on the hour. It was located at the end of Avenue Kakh, where the ex-Shah's palace was. Martha was really excited. After spending all that time acclimatizing herself to the environment and the spirits on Planet Heaven, she was finally on her way to meet Bizet. Martha's mission was to let Bizet know of his great fame on Earth after his death. For some reason she thought Georges must have no inkling about how much people of the world liked his works, especially his opera *Carmen*.

As they were walking toward the escalator, Sooren said, "Hurry, Martha. The escalator going to America will be starting to roll within a few seconds."

Martha was totally taken aback by Sooren's words "Uncle Sooren," she protested, "you never mentioned anything about a trip to America. Besides, doesn't Georges Bizet live in France?

"Yes. But, we are first going to America."

"May I ask why?"

"Well, it's a surprise."

"Oh my! I can't wait to find out!" Martha said, rubbing the palms of her hands together. She normally did that when she was about to do something exciting.

Martha grinned and said, "Now I know why you were after me so much to stop talking to Marie! You were impatient to get me out so we could head to America."

Sooren chuckled impishly but did not speak, which made it even more interesting for Martha.

Soon they both trudged onto the first step of the escalator as it began rolling upward through a dense cloud.

The clouds at first felt thick, dark, and moist. However, as they advanced farther upward, the clouds seemed to be fluffy and weightless. Martha gradually could perceive some rays of bright light piercing through the clouds. Suddenly, the escalator came to a jolting stop. She almost fell flat upon her face, but Uncle Sooren grabbed her arm and steadied her.

Soon, they found themselves in a busy square crowded with cafés, restaurants, malls, and dance halls. A blaring sound of rock 'n' roll music pierced the air. Martha looked astounded. "It sounds like Elvis; am I correct?"

"Yes, you are, my dear. That was the surprise I had in store for you. I always knew how much you liked his music." He beamed and continued, "And, of course, you know that we are now on American soil."

"You must be joking! Already?"

"No, there are no jokes involved. This is really America, the heavenly United States."

He tapped his hand against Martha's shoulder tenderly. "We'll soon go and listen to Elvis, and then travel to another level where God's throne is located."

Martha said, "Oh dear. You are really spoiling me. Uncle Sooren, you haven't changed at all!"

Then, she looked straight ahead into a busy hall with an open door. She saw Elvis singing, "Only You," rolling his hips and moving his legs to the rhythm of his song.

Martha began humming along as she rushed inside to say hello to Elvis. He looked exactly like in his younger days, with his long sideburns; dark, greased hair; tight white pants; and silver, high-collared jacket with rhinestones. Young boys and girls dressed in colorful sixties-style costumes swayed and twisted to Elvis's music.

Soon, Uncle Sooren and Martha had joined the crowd and begun dancing too. Martha noticed that on Planet Heaven, age was immaterial. People of all ages easily mingled together.

Elvis now finished his song and stared at Martha while wearing a broad smile on his face. Walking toward her, he said, "Welcome to Planet Heaven, Martha."

"Thank you," Martha said as she extended her hand to Elvis.

Then she walked closer to her uncle and whispered into his ear, "How does he know my name?"

"Look up there on the large computerized screen." Sooren pointed to the opposite wall.

Martha saw with great surprise her name written across the top of the screen, along with the names of other newcomers to Planet Heaven.

Elvis looked at Martha as he fiddled around with the chords of his white gleaming guitar and asked, "Have you already been to Heaven?"

Uncle Sooren interjected before Martha had a chance to answer, "That's where we're headed next."

"OK. That's fine, but first, try to have fun here with us."

Martha smiled from ear to ear and answered, "You bet! On Earth, I could never sit still anytime I heard your music playing. I had to dance, shake, rock 'n' roll, and sing along with your music, no matter what age. And now it's for real!"

Chapter 29

The Heaven

Farther down the alley, there was an exceptionally long and steep escalator gliding upward and disappearing into a dense fog.

At first, the stairs revolved at regular pace, the way they do at department stores. Then unexpectedly, Martha and Sooren found themselves grabbing hard at the banister of the speeding escalator to avoid tumbling off. They really were moving at a dizzying speed. Martha closed her eyes and tried to keep calm. She was beginning to feel giddy and did not like that sensation.

Sooren said, "Hold on to me; otherwise, you'll flip backward." Martha immediately obeyed him, with her eyes still closed.

To take her mind off the scary, fast-moving stairs, Martha began thinking about the family members she had just met. She also pondered the possibility of meeting the saints as well as Jesus. "Uncle," Martha asked, "I was wondering if we could meet Jesus in heaven."

Fortunately, it was a Tuesday. On Tuesdays, Jesus entertained friends and visitors starting at two o'clock in the afternoon.

After a few minutes, the escalator came to a shuddering stop. Martha stumbled forward, which forced her eyes open. To her great amazement, she saw a shimmering gate giving way to a luscious green patch of land.

Before stepping into the glorious garden, with aromatic and exotic colorful flowers, vibrant bushes, all kinds of large and small trees, Martha heard a dog barking right behind her. She turned around and was flabbergasted to find her beloved pet, Shoonik, her jet-black, handsome German shepherd. The moment Shoonik realized that Martha had noticed him, he began barking louder and wagging his tail like a propeller.

"Goodness! It's you, my lovely Shoonik!" Martha shrieked with joy, as her eyes glowed radiantly. Shoonik had been Martha's loyal friend and companion after her father's death. Martha remembered how painful it had been for her to separate from Shoonik when she was eleven years old. This had happened when Martha's family had to sell their magnificent house in Arak in order to move to Tehran. Her two older brothers had found jobs in Tehran and rented an apartment. They had arranged for Martha, her younger brother, and their mother to join them. Lily, Martha's sister, was living in Tehran with Uncle Sooren and Aunt Hasmik while studying at Tehran University.

Unfortunately, the owner of the apartment in Tehran strictly forbade them to bring along any pets. So, they had no other choice than to give Martha's beloved pet away to a village lord. Martha suffered immensely in those days for having given up her darling Shoonik. And now, finally, here she was reunited with her loyal friend.

Shoonik seemed happy to see Martha, too. He pounced up, stood on his hind legs, and placed his paws on her shoulders as he licked her face.

"Shoonik, I am so happy you found me. I'll never leave you anymore. I promise you. Yes, I want you to be with me forever. You are my best buddy!"

Martha wiped her tears and uttered, "Shoonik, I love you so much!"

Chapter 30

Beloved Shoonik

Martha mused about her childhood days with Shoonik. She remembered how after Gregor had passed away, the dog became her protector from nasty Persian boys who chased her and sang offensive anti-Armenian rhymes. They shamelessly insulted a helpless ten-year-old girl just because she was a Christian and not a Muslim. This normally would happen in the afternoon, on her way home from school. Shoonik would wait for her by their gate every day around four thirty. The Persian boys, too, would lie in wait for Martha to show up at Gerdoo Street, where Martha lived. As soon as they set their eyes upon her, they would begin to annoy her with their ridiculous remarks. Martha would call out at the top of her voice, "Shoonik, come and get these boys!"

Shoonik, upon hearing Martha's voice, would dart across the street like an arrow, attack the boys, and scatter them away. Martha was so happy that she had such a great protector. Now, here he was again, just in case she needed his help. Martha couldn't have asked for anything better! Finding

Shoonik looking so healthy, so young, and so well on Planet Heaven was like the best gift ever!

Shoonik continued licking Martha's hands and face. It was obvious that he had missed her tremendously. Uncle Sooren smiled. "This is the best thing that could ever happen to you. It is very exciting!"

Martha patted her dog on the head and said, "Shoonik, you have to travel to France with us to help us find Georges Bizet."

The dog cocked his head and uttered joyous noises.

"You mean yes, don't you?" Martha exclaimed happily.

In response, Shoonik began wagging his tail rhythmically as he pulled his ears back. Martha was familiar with that look from old times. When Shoonik drew his ears back, he was contented. Of course, if he did the same gesture with those nasty boys back on Earth, he was angry and ready to attack.

A few moments later, a young man of medium height with an unshaven face, long hair pulled back in a ponytail, and sparkling dark eyes ran forward and said hello to Martha. "Do you remember me?" he asked.

Martha rubbed her chin in contemplation as the man continued. "Of course, you must. I am that homeless man who lived in upper Manhattan. I asked you for a dollar to get myself a cup of coffee."

Martha slapped her forehead. "Yes, of course. How could I forget such a gallant person?"

Martha remembered how she had been walking on Broadway on a Sunday morning on her way to church. As she was about a block away from the church, a homeless man approached her and asked for a dollar to buy a cup of coffee.

Martha drew out two dollars from her purse and offered the bills to the fellow.

He'd smiled and said, "Thank you. Thank you so much! Can I invite you for coffee?"

Martha's heart was filled with compassion and appreciation of such a chivalrous person. She thought that one rarely comes across such impressive people with big hearts.

Martha smiled at him warmly and answered, "Thanks for your kind offer, but I'm on my way to church. It will begin in five minutes; otherwise, I would have accepted your invitation."

The man asked, "Can I go to church with you?"

"Of course, you can! A church is God's house and is open to everyone who wishes to attend."

The homeless man followed Martha to church, but when they entered the impressive-looking sanctuary, he looked around him. The sight of all the well-dressed people and the rich environment, as well as the decor, intimidated this poor, shabbily dressed fellow. He turned around and exited the church at the speed of sound.

Martha shook the homeless man's hand in Heaven happily and asked, "By the way, despite the fact that I recognize you, I have no clue what your name is."

"George. George Simpson."

"Wow!" Martha said. "What a coincidence. Do you know that I am going to search for the composer Georges Bizet on Planet Heaven? He is the same person who composed the opera *Carmen*. How interesting that your name is George, too…although his name is spelled the French way, ending in the letter *s*."

George laughed. "Well, unfortunately, I'm not the same person. Good luck in finding him." George waved his hand good-bye and disappeared as quickly as he had in church that day on Earth.

Martha laughed, shook her head, and said, "How lovely! He was a strange man on planet Earth, and he seems to be the same up here. He hasn't changed a bit."

Chapter 31

What a Fun Life

Sooren and Martha enjoyed their promenade through the lush green path, which led to a shiny glass palace. Some distance away, to the right of the majestic building, a deep ravine further embellished the picturesque valley with its mighty waterfall, which spilled its roaring water into a choppy river. Meanwhile, myriad heavenly birds chirped and sang melodiously as they soared in circles high above the waterfall. Along the road, yellow, blue, green, and purple butterflies merrily danced around butterfly bushes, covered in white flowers. Martha drank in the beauty of the surroundings as she turned to Shoonik, who was following behind. She was curious to know what his reaction to the vibrant atmosphere of the glorious heavenly garden was. To her great surprise, her pet seemed to be unimpressed. She realized that this might be nothing new to him. He had been on Planet Heaven for a long time, so nothing was as novel to him, the way it was to Martha.

After a short walk, Sooren and Martha found themselves in front of a set of sliding glass doors, which gave way to the palace. The glass doors rolled open immediately as they stepped over the threshold. The extreme brightness of the hall was blinding. Shoonik whined and abruptly rushed outside. Sooren and Martha covered their eyes with their hands.

"We have to get used to this bright, holy light. Take a deep breath, and count to ten," Sooren whispered. "Then open your eyes gradually. Remember, I said gradually. Otherwise, you'll become blind for a whole day."

Martha did as Sooren had instructed her, and slowly, she was able to see her surroundings with ease. Martha was shocked to behold the walls covered with gigantic computer screens, somewhat similar to the ones at airports but ten times larger. Martha noticed millions of names typed on those screens, which kept scrolling down as new names showed up on top.

"What are all those names typed on those enormous computer screens?" Martha asked.

"Those are the names of the people due to arrive to Heaven in the next coming days and weeks."

Martha made a great effort to read them. She wished to find out if there were any familiar names. She had never been a fast reader, though, and with the rapid speed with which the names on the screens flew by, it was almost impossible for her to follow them.

Soon, the sound of a restful melody permeated the huge chamber with its shiny, black marble floors. The angelic and soothing music, which to Martha sounded like the tranquil flow of a smooth river, rendered her with a feeling of deep serenity. It had been a while since she had experienced such a heavenly, peaceful, and wonderful sensation. She fixed her eyes at the end of the immense, awe-inspiring chamber and noticed four long steps leading to another set of imposing sliding glass doors.

This second entrance opened up into another grand hall. When the doors glided open, Sooren and Martha saw a huge rectangular table covered with delicious-looking foods in the middle of the room. A large group of men and women sat around the table, eating happily and drinking some wine.

At that point, the tune of the existing melody switched from a soothing classical composition to a cheerful country-music song. The words rang out, "Me and Jesus had our own thing going." Martha wondered who the disc jockey in Heaven could be. It might be one of the past famous radio presenters! Then she mused, *We've heard all kinds of nice music, including classical, but nothing from Georges Bizet.*

At that moment, the joyous melody took her back to Westhampton, where she had driven around the surrounding villages and towns in her red convertible Mercedes-Benz with its black top down. Martha was driving toward Hampton Bays one day when she'd heard that same country song for the first time on the radio. Martha loved it. She could not stop swaying to its joyous rhythm while she drove. Yes, it was indeed a cheerful song. Martha was enchanted to think that Planet Heaven was similar to Earth in so many ways. She told herself again that if people on Earth knew about this, they would never be afraid of dying.

Uncle Sooren held on to Martha's hand and pulled her forward to introduce her to a white-robed man with long, wavy brown hair. He tapped on the man's shoulder to get his attention. When the man turned around, Martha was stunned to see it was Jesus himself. His kind, loving eyes stared at her. She was surprised to see that he looked no different from the depiction on all the paintings she had seen by modern and classical artists through the centuries.

Jesus stood, shook Martha's and Sooren's hands, and pulled two chairs out for them to sit down. Wearing a friendly smile upon his face, he said, "Hi, Martha, glad to meet you. Welcome! I'm really happy to see you here."

Jesus then called out, "Mother…Mother, could you bring a jug of water, please?"

Martha wondered why Jesus wanted the Holy Mother to bring some water. Did they have to wash their hands according to tradition? In Jesus's time, Israelites would bring out a jug of water and a bowl to have their guests rinse their hands before eating.

Mary appeared in no time wearing a white shawl, which wrapped loosely around her head and shoulders. She had a gentle and loving smile. Under her arm she carried a large glass jug of water. Placing the container on the table, the Holy Mother gazed at Martha and her uncle. Sooren and Martha, meanwhile, clambered to their feet, stooped, and kissed Mary's hand with great reverence. Her warmth and compassion streamed out around her, like rays emanating from the powerful, nurturing sun. When Mary placed the jug on the table, Jesus pressed his mother to his chest and kissed her head, saying, "Mother, would you like to join us, to greet our new guest from Earth?"

Mary observed Martha through a pair of almond-shaped blue eyes and said, "No, thanks. I have a lot of work to attend to." Then, smiling warmly, she asked Martha, "What's your name?"

Martha looked down at her hands shyly and responded, "Martha, Holy Mother."

"Welcome, Martha. Welcome, and enjoy your wine."

What wine is she referring to? I don't see any around, Martha asked herself, assuming that the jug of clear water was simply for washing hands.

As soon as Mary strode away, Jesus laid a hand upon the jug and prayed. Martha was shocked to see the water turn into ruby-red wine within seconds. Jesus then beckoned Sooren and Martha to regain their seats. He filled their glasses with the miracle wine. "I'm sure you need a good drink to relax. You must be very tired from your long journey."

Chapter 32

Gohar—A Real Surprise

While Martha was busy enjoying her superb glass of wine, the likes of which she had never tasted before, she thought about Zaven, who, being a real wine connoisseur, would have appreciated this fabulous elixir. Martha told herself that she must make sure to bring Zaven to visit Jesus when he eventually arrived on Planet Heaven. *Indeed*, she pondered, *it would be a sin to deprive him of such a precious experience.*

At that instance, an elderly woman with an unsteady gait approached Jesus, interrupting Martha's thoughts. The woman appeared to be drunk, the way she fixed her drowsy eyes upon Jesus and wobbled on her feet. She came closer and asked, slurring her words, "Dear Jesus, could you kindly give me a glass of your nice wine? Please? I'm really thirsty."

Her slim figure, green eyes, and pale complexion seemed familiar to Martha. *She might be a relative*, Martha thought to herself. Sooren, too, looked at her curiously. Martha suspected that her uncle also could be pondering whether she was related to them.

Jesus turned around, smiled at the woman, and uttered, "Oh, it's you again, Gohar." He then smiled fondly and continued, "I can see you are back for more drinks, aren't you?"

"Did he say Gohar?" Martha mumbled quietly to herself as Sooren shifted uncomfortably in his seat. The name definitely was familiar to her.

In the meantime, Gohar fixed her dozy eyes at Jesus and slurred, "Please, Master, may I have some wine?"

Martha suspected that the stranger might be none other than her great-grandmother Gohar, who was a drunkard on planet Earth all through her lifetime. Anoosh, Martha's mother, often told stories about her grandmother Gohar. Apparently, Gohar always embarrassed her children in front of their friends. Anoosh explained that Gohar had a son, Manuel, who had been educated in the United States. After returning to Hamadan from New York, he had invited one of his friends home for a cup of tea. That day Gohar had been wickedly drunk. She had gone around using foul language and behaving badly.

Manuel had told her, "Mother, please behave yourself! You are humiliating me."

"Just shut up, you no-good punk! Who do you think you are?" she had barked wildly.

Her uncle's expression confirmed to Martha that Gohar was indeed his maternal grandmother. She also was well aware that Sooren had never met Gohar on Earth because she had died before his birth. Martha hoped that Uncle Sooren would get up and introduce her and himself to Gohar, but he seemed none too keen to do so.

He could be feeling embarrassed in front of Jesus, she thought. But didn't Jesus already know of her relationship to Sooren and Martha? Of course he did. He simply didn't want to encourage the woman to stay on, which could mean that she would insist on having more drinks.

Taking on a somber look, Jesus told Gohar, "Sorry, my dear lady, you have been drinking all day long. I think you should not have any more wine. I really mean it, Gohar. That's enough! Please go back to your room, and try to sleep."

He then shook his head and murmured to himself, "I shouldn't have allowed her to come back for more drinks earlier."

"But, Master, I'm thirsty," she protested.

"Why don't you drink some cold water? It might sober you up. Go on; do as you're told," Jesus said firmly but affectionately as Gohar staggered away.

As Martha's eyes followed her great-grandmother, she wondered how Gohar would have acted had she found out who she and Sooren were. Most probably, Gohar would have gaped at them and told them to go to hell. That's the kind of woman she had been on Earth.

Chapter 33

Technology in Heaven

Jesus read Martha's mind about Gohar, beheld her with great affection, and smiled. Martha's heart overflowed with love, and her whole being glowed with a sense of glory. Jesus, knowing about Martha's feelings, simply nodded to confirm her thoughts. Now Martha could guess why Jesus had not introduced his two visitors to Gohar. He indeed did not wish to create an uncomfortable situation. If Gohar had been sober, the situation would have been different.

Spending time with Jesus that day and comprehending his deep compassion for his guests, Martha thought of her own love for Jesus. When she was a little girl, almost every night she had dreamed of him as a friend, a kind man who cherished children and mended their broken dolls. Those dreams always were extremely pleasing, which made her wake up with a special fun mood every morning. Martha also thought about all the miracles that had taken place during her life on Earth. She recalled that whenever she prayed to Jesus with real faith, her prayers were answered without exception. She understood that it was all a question of faith. Anybody praying with great hope to their prophets or to God could receive a positive response. The other thing that Martha claimed was that on certain occasions, she had been lucky to feel a holy presence.

At that instance, Martha looked at Jesus with great admiration and said, "Thank you for all the help you rendered me when I prayed to you during my difficult times throughout my childhood and life on Earth."

Jesus placed a friendly hand on Martha's shoulder and responded, "I'm here to help those who ask me with faith."

"How can you handle billions of prayers?" Martha asked. "To me, it all seems impossible!"

Jesus suddenly took on a serious demeanor. He stared musingly at Martha and uttered, "The computer technicians and operators sort out the most urgent prayer requests and e-mail them to me."

"This is very interesting! I had no idea of the way you handled prayers." Martha grinned. "It is fascinating that here on Planet Heaven, like on Earth, technology plays such a great role."

"Yes, we were computerized way back before people on Earth began thinking about technology. To add to my comments about answering prayers, I must stress that all prayers get a response, but in the order of urgency."

Chapter 34

Her Prayers Answered

Martha told herself, *so that's how my wishes would come true on Earth!*

All through her life, whenever Martha needed assistance in solving a problem or receiving something almost impossible, she used to meditate with great concentration. Martha tried to empty her mind of all worldly thoughts and prayed. If she was lucky, she would enter an unusual spiritual realm similar to a stupor or trance. It was within boundaries of such a mental awareness that Martha believed she accomplished her purpose of attracting God's attention. Thus, in her spiritual world, she would plead with Him to help her with her difficulty. Without exception, Martha's wish would be fulfilled through prayer. Martha claimed that during the days of her life on Earth, especially when she was a little girl, she could open up a direct, invisible telephone line to God.

Whenever Martha prayed and asked Him for something with real faith and power of meditation, she always received it. Wasn't it amazing that her mother bought Martha that special stuffed kitten without her even uttering a word about her desire to possess one? They had no money at the time. She was almost nine years old, and her father had been deceased for almost a year. So to receive the things they could not afford to buy, she prayed persistently. Yes, even at the age of nine, Martha believed that God received her "telephone calls" and granted her everything for which she asked.

As a married woman, Martha achieved connecting with God through the same method. Yes, there were times when Martha felt upset, requiring assistance to solve a certain dilemma. She turned to her Lord, whom she liked to call the Almighty, or the awesome, noble, and mysterious power. Sure enough—when Martha prayed fervently, she believed that the mighty, invisible power came to her rescue. Meanwhile, Martha was not a typical Christian who accepted everything blindly. She was simply a believer. She mostly believed in goodness: good energy, good thoughts, and love—all of which Jesus taught. What's more, she ardently held the opinion that people should try to strengthen the Good Generator, or the good energy in the world, with their upright conduct.

Numerous impossible events were solved for Martha on Earth, which could easily be considered miraculous. One such example had happened during Martha's and her family's dwelling in the village of Monnetier-Mornex, not too far from the town of Annemasse in France. During that time, they still held Iranian citizenship, so in order to renew their passports, they were forced to drive to the bordering city of Geneva in Switzerland. Unfortunately, embassies and consulates did not have offices in the small town of Annemasse.

After the family had lived in France for two years, Zaven's company transferred him to England. Thus, he and the children moved to a hotel in the United Kingdom. Martha had stayed behind to organize the packing of their household goods and the move. A few days earlier, she had taken her passport to the Iranian Consulate in Geneva to have it renewed. Martha was supposed to pick it up the day before her departure to the United Kingdom. Had Zaven been around, he would have fetched the passport for her.

Normally, the border guards in Annemasse never checked the cars entering France from Switzerland, so someone without a passport didn't face a major problem. The authorities in the town of Annemasse were pleased to have tourists enter their town. The Swiss guards did not seem to care much about the cars leaving their country but required drivers to go through the checkpoint to enter Switzerland.

The day before her departure to England, Martha headed to the border to attempt the drive into Geneva. When she arrived at the border, to her great dismay, she found a long line of cars waiting to be inspected before entering Switzerland. Martha stared with apprehension at the two stern-looking officers in their gray uniforms. Without exception, they stopped every car and checked the passports. The border guards also inspected the trunks. Martha suspected they were searching for drugs.

Martha panicked when she noticed the Swiss guards' unrelenting efforts. She told herself that those officers undoubtedly would stop her from entering Switzerland without a passport, even if she explained the reason she didn't have one.

She closed her eyes and prayed passionately. She asked Jesus to come and sit next to her and help her cross the border. After her prayer was over, she suddenly felt a feeling of complete relaxation. Martha sat back serenely and awaited her turn. She thought that if the guards stopped her from entering Geneva because of not having her passport, Martha could show them the receipt issued by the Iranian Consulate. Perhaps they could ask her to sign a special form and let her through.

Presently, the Swiss guards finished checking the car ahead of her. As Martha rolled her window down and prepared to stop, the Swiss border guards beckoned her to drive on and enter Geneva. Martha was astonished to see the next car being stopped immediately. She was indeed flabbergasted and could not believe her luck.

Once in Geneva, she pulled over to the shoulder of the road, turned to the invisible passenger next to her, as if he were really present, and said, "Thank you, Jesus, for helping me cross the border." Truly, Martha was so happy that she could not help laughing and talking to herself out loud. She watched the border through her rearview mirror for a while and noticed that the guards again stopped all the cars for inspection without exception.

Chapter 35

An Interesting Discorse

"Do you have any plans on Planet Heaven?" Jesus asked, jolting Martha out of her reverie.

"Yes, I would first like to find Georges Bizet. Once I succeed and figure out what he is up to on this planet, I will think about a specific profession I can follow on Planet Heaven."

Jesus said, "Oh, you mean you're going to look for the nineteenth-century French composer?"

"Yes, my Lord. My plan was to immediately start my search for Bizet, but Uncle Sooren thought it would be better to first explore Planet Heaven a bit more before our trip to France to look for Bizet."

"Have you seen enough?"

Martha said, "I am sure there is plenty more to see, but I would like to go ahead fulfilling my plan."

"Any reason for wanting to find this musician?" he asked, arching his eyebrows quizzically.

Martha's eyes shone like two diamonds with excitement, feeling flattered that Jesus would be interested in her plan. *Maybe*, she thought, *he can help me find George Bizet.*

Martha took a deep breath and said, "Bizet has no idea that he is so famous on Earth. I would really like to inform him about that. Besides, thinking about his suffering on Earth has always saddened me."

Martha sighed and continued, "I myself went through the same kind of painful experience as Bizet, when I was younger and trying to get published."

"That's right. The poor man was devastated when he read about the cruel reviews after the first performance of *Carmen*."

"Yes, my Lord," Martha confirmed.

Jesus nodded approvingly and said, "You seem like a caring person. That's a good trait. I'm all for it."

"Let's hope I can succeed."

"I can help you find him, if you wish." Jesus suggested.

Martha looked down, smiled sheepishly, and said, "Actually, I was about to ask you my Lord but decided that it would be nicer if I try to find Bizet all by myself."

Jesus patted Martha on the shoulder approvingly.

Suddenly, it occurred to Martha to ask, "Why is it that on Planet Heaven, we hear all kinds of music being played but nothing by Bizet?"

"You are right. I wonder why our broadcaster does not include his music in his repertoire!"

Martha narrowed her eyes in contemplation. "Yes, indeed. How can it be that such a great musician's work is being ignored on Planet Heaven?"

Jesus shrugged. Martha could tell that he had never thought about this before.

Switching to a different subject, Martha said, "What I would like to talk about has nothing to do with the subject of my search for Bizet, but I suddenly remembered how before my arrival to Planet Heaven, people on different parts of Earth were suffering from the consequences of terrorism."

She coughed to clear her scratchy throat and continued. "I am so curious to hear about your thoughts about such harrowing deeds."

"You mean incidents such as the attacks on September 11, 2001, the Boston Marathon bombing, the explosions in Iraq, and the cruel actions of different Islamic fundamentalist groups such as ISIS?"

"Yes, as well as the Oklahoma City bombing in the past and other failed bombing attempts."

Martha took a deep breath, sighed, and continued. "I'm referring to the terrible conduct of both Muslim and Christian fundamentalists. Our Christian militants are as dangerous as Muslim extremists."

"I know. Prophet Muhammad and I often meet and talk about those sad events. When we were still living on Earth, both of us preached about tolerance and humanity. Unfortunately, in today's world, there are some sly, self-interested religious leaders in both religions who fill simple-minded people's hearts and minds with hatred and bigotry."

"Can't you both try to influence such people and help them to change?" Martha asked.

"We do try. Unfortunately, they won't hear us. It really breaks our hearts that because of freedom of choice existing on Earth, we are sometimes powerless." He sighed and added, "Yet both of us agree that it is good for people to think the way they wish and act as they please, as long as they don't harm one another."

Jesus's face clouded. He stared at Martha and continued. "What extremists do today is contrary to Prophet Muhammad's teachings. He taught his followers that they should respect Jews and Christians and allow those religions to practice freely in Muslim countries. But look at ISIS, for example. They behead or shoot people who don't accept Islam the way they want them to. They even kill kind and charitable individuals who travel all the way to countries such as Syria for humanitarian purposes. Yes, their behavior is despicable! It really saddens Prophet Muhammad to know that these extremists commit such violent acts under his name. To make things worse, such scary groups wish to take over the whole world and force people to become like them."

Jesus looked down at his sandals, shook his head, and said, "I always pray for such people to reform, to see the light, and to have their minds opened."

Chapter 36

The TV Evangelists

Martha had another question. "What do you think about Christian TV evangelists who use your name to gain tons of money and conduct a luxurious life? They shamelessly take advantage of simple people, sometimes even those with meager means."

Jesus shook his head as his eyes welled with tears. "It is really sad! I can't understand such opportunists."

"True," Martha agreed. "And when the news media reproaches them with questions like 'How do you explain your lavish lifestyle?' they answer that it is for the glory of God. Ridiculous, isn't it? Come to think of it, dear Jesus, when you lived on Earth, you didn't even have a proper roof over your head! You lived like a gypsy, didn't you?"

Jesus smiled, remembering his past life with his friends and followers on Earth.

"You are right. We all shared whatever we had in order to be able to survive. We shared food and everything together.

Taking advantage of the nice weather in Israel, we mostly slept outdoors."

While Jesus talked with Martha and Sooren, he turned to his right, toward a large computer screen installed in the wall. He then pressed a hidden button under the table, sliding out a keyboard. He switched on the computer and clicked on a specific link. Finding what he was looking for, Jesus said, "Here. Let's watch this."

Chapter 37

A Brilliant Servant

The computer showed a YouTube video about a preacher. He looked like he would be in his mid to late forties. He was of medium height and reasonably good-looking with dark, greased hair and dark eyes.

"Master, he is supposed to be your servant. Your *billionaire* servant," Martha told Jesus. "Just look at his thousands of acres of land, with the palatial mansion built right in the center of his property!"

Sooren added, "And look at his ultramodern jet and private airfield. Where do you think he got all that money to acquire his luxuries belongings?"

"Where else?" Martha answered. "He accumulated all that money from simple and innocent people, like a widow friend of mine who could hardly make ends meet!"

Sooren sighed. "I know exactly who you are talking about. I'm also aware that she zealously believes in what this man preaches. She goes around proselytizing for this charlatan."

Jesus, Sooren, and Martha listened attentively to the video as a reporter asked the minister, "Why do you need a private jet and your own airfield?"

The minister looked the reporter straight in the eyes and said, "To better serve the Lord."

Martha interjected, "Who serves the Lord better—a poor monk with worn-out sandals and bare necessities or a jet-owning preacher?"

Jesus smiled and said, "I really like your astute ideas about such human behavior. If we had billions of people like you, Sooren, and those reporters on Earth, things would be different."

They discontinued their conversation to listen to another question from the reporter on the video: "Why don't you answer my questions truthfully? I'm asking you some simple questions."

"Ask again. I will give you simple answers."

"Well, again, why do you need to have such a luxurious style of life? Aren't preachers supposed to be humble servants of God?"

"My lifestyle," he said, "is according to the Scriptures."

The minister then turned his back to the reporter and walked away, accompanied by his bodyguards.

Jesus looked disappointed. It was obvious that he was frustrated to listen to such hypocrites who used him to build themselves an empire.

Martha was furious. "What does he think? Does the stupid guy believe that we are *all* fools?"

Sooren also seemed angry. He stood and began pacing the space behind Jesus's chair. "They also call themselves faith healers," he said. "They pretend that like you, dear Jesus, they have the healing power."

Sooren explained that these evangelists typically gather a large group in a hall or a church and begin preaching. They tell naïve Christians that in order for them to be healed of their ailments, they need to pay some money to be used for God's glory.

Sooren appeared really frustrated and said, "Glory! What do these abusers mean by *God's glory*?"

Martha interjected, "What they mean is to use God's name to fill their pockets. The shameless impostors!"

Sooren cut in as Jesus listened pensively. "After this so-called healer asks a sick person to drop a certain amount of money into the collection tray, his aides guide him or her onto the pulpit while the healer begins praying and yelling and making strange noises."

"Afterward, the 'healer' lays hand on the forehead of the sick individual as two or three men stand behind the person to catch him or her as he violently pushes the poor soul to the ground," Martha said. "Then when the poor prey stands up, the preacher stops praying and asks if she or he feels all right. From being pushed down, the person's body gets a rush of adrenaline, so he or she immediately but temporarily feels pain-free."

Sooren added that the sick person in question then gets up and begins praising the Lord for having healed her or him of terrible illnesses. However, after a few hours, the poor victim's problems return.

Chapter 38

The Pope

Martha asked Jesus, "Do you approve of Pope Francis?"

"Oh yes. He is one of the greatest leaders in Christianity. I believe he is going to reform the Catholic Church. He will help his bishops and the church members to get enlightened."

"Indeed," Martha said. "What I like the most about him is that contrary to all the fundamentalist Christian leaders, he believes in treating people of different faiths with respect."

Jesus gazed at Martha expectantly.

"For example," Martha continued, "he participates at services held at different synagogues in the honor of the Jewish Holocaust victims. The pope also holds meetings with some progressive-minded Muslim religious leaders. He believes that all religions are good."

Sooren nodded and added, "Unfortunately, conventional and backward-looking Christians blame the pope for his broadmindedness. They don't respect him because he is not as conservative as previous popes. These ignorant people don't think that this kind of behavior will help promote peace among people around the world, which, in my opinion, should be a requirement in real Christianity."

Martha cut in. "Yes. I totally agree with you. The other thing that I like about Pope Francis is that contrary to most Catholic religious authorities, he suggests that even homosexuals, single mothers, and divorced couples should not be excluded from the Catholic Church."

Sooren said, "True; he is indeed different. Don't you like his statement made a while back about animals going to Heaven, because of being God's creations?"

Martha interjected, "Yes; the reason for his comment was to comfort a little boy who had lost his beloved dog. Anyway, he is not wrong. How about my Shoonik? He's in Heaven with us."

Jesus smiled and nodded approvingly as he looked into the distance, appearing to be a bit distracted. Martha wished she had the ability to read Jesus's mind. In the meantime, she told herself that all through her life, like the present pope, she had had an open mind regarding tolerance and respect for people of different religions. Martha disagreed with those who claimed that in order for a person to enter the kingdom of God, he or she had to be a Christian. Instead, she was convinced that all good human beings belonging to the goodness in the world that she called the Good Generator were God's children. Therefore, how could God punish them for believing in their own prophets rather than Jesus? Besides, she believed that there were millions and millions of evildoers among Christians. People such as gangsters, drug dealers, and the like, still attended church and prayed despite all their criminal deeds. Did it mean that such people, simply because they prayed to Jesus, would go to Heaven? She was sure that the pope, like her, believed that an upright and pious Muslim, Buddhist, or a Jewish person was no different from any respectable Christian in God's sight.

Chapter 39

A Surprise Visitor

Martha and Sooren prepared to say good-bye to Jesus. Suddenly, a tall, long-robed man with white hair, a gray beard, and a large and lengthy staff walked into the room. Jesus immediately rushed to his feet and bowed to the man. He said, "Martha and Sooren, please meet the holy and honorable Moses."

Both Sooren and Martha instantly followed suit. They were speechless. They could have never dreamed of having such an honor as to encounter a holy figure like Prophet Moses. In the meantime, Martha wondered where Prophet Muhammad could be. She told herself that because of the present terrorist activities and cruelties, he likely was extremely busy working hard to pacify Muslims concerning their acceptance of Jews and Christians living in the Middle East. Martha sighed, thinking how these special sects of Muslims tried to force their religion upon non-Muslims by the might of their daggers. Indeed, for them, if you did not convert to Islam, you deserved to die. The massacre of one and a half million Armenians by the Ottoman Empire was partly an example of such behavior.

Martha thought that she would also love to meet with Buddha. *We have lots of opportunities to do so*, *after I have found George Bizet*, she convinced herself.

Moses's deep and manly voice interrupted Martha's thoughts. "Sit down. Sit down," he said.

He pulled up a chair, sat down, and stated, "While I was walking by, I couldn't help but to overhear your conversation. Would you like to hear my point of view?"

They all, including Jesus, said in unison, "Of course, Prophet Moses!"

"When I was leading the Israelites out of Egypt, although I was doing everything in my power to serve my people and introduce them to the mercy of God, some of them turned against Him. Did I do something wrong? Was it entirely my fault?"

Jesus shook his head. "No, of course not."

"Well, instead of them being thankful to God for His mercy in getting them out of Egypt and being freed from slavery, they turned arrogant and forgot about their heavenly Father. They built idols for themselves and began worshiping them.

"Again, I always wonder what I did wrong. I know that I shouldn't have lost my temper. Indeed, I should not have smashed the tablets of the Ten Commandments out of anger…"

Neither Jesus nor Martha nor Sooren uttered a word. Martha and Sooren especially thought it was not their place to speak.

"What I'm trying to relay is that humans are vulnerable beings," Moses said. "No matter what their prophets preach or teach them, some go their own way and follow their vices."

Jesus confirmed, "Yes, you are right. Some of my followers not only use my name to benefit themselves, but instead of loving one another—instead of showing respect toward other religions—they commit horrible acts, such as burning a Koran and so forth."

"Yes," Moses said. "I agree. Come to think of it, even though you taught that your followers are supposed to love their enemies as well as their neighbors, some act like pagans."

Moses sighed and added, "Unfortunately, neither my people nor Jesus's followers nor Muslims behave accordingly." He shook his head a few times. "Ignorance!"

Jesus nodded as Sooren and Martha listened attentively. Then, having spoken his mind, Moses got up and strode away.

Chapter 40

It Is All The Same

Martha suddenly thought of Zaven. She told herself, *This is the kind of discussion that Zaven would love. In fact, so would Haroot and Sylvia.*

Martha was very proud to think of how liberal minded both her children were.

The memory of Zaven and her two children made Martha long for them for the hundredth time since her arrival in Heaven. Jesus gazed at her compassionately with a warm and loving smile. He could sense Martha's feelings. Martha blinked her tears away. She then scrambled to her feet and said, "My Lord, Jesus, I am honored to have met you in Heaven and to have had the pleasure of speaking with you."

Sooren also stood, bowed to Jesus, and followed Martha out of the large hall. When they got outside, they saw Shoonik awaiting them by the sliding doors, sleeping peacefully with his head resting on his paws.

"Which way to France, Uncle Sooren? Can you please check it on your iPhone?"

Martha had hardly opened her mouth before Shoonik awoke, sprang upon his feet, and raced ahead toward the direction of the woods, just like a missile.

"There," Sooren said. "He knows better than any sophisticated electronic device the right way to France. Hurry up. Let's follow Shoonik as fast as we can, before we lose this speedy creature."

Chapter 41

Heading Toward France

Shoonik virtually flew through the woods, making it hard for Martha and Sooren to keep pace with him. The trees zoomed by on both sides of the path at a dizzying speed. The deer, large geese, and wild turkey grazing among the grass came across as blurs. The pleasant air swishing in their ears sounded like an outer-space melody. This convinced Martha that the atmosphere surrounding them was filled with a background of unusually nerve-soothing, soft energy.

In no time, Shoonik, Martha, and Uncle Sooren zipped out of the forest and landed on their feet in a spacious pasture. Martha noticed the silhouette of a cluster of buildings, which resembled a large city from a distance.

"Look over there, Uncle Sooren!" Martha said.

"Yes, I can see. It must be the bordering city in France."

Shoonik barked and sped ahead. Sooren urged, "Listen, Martha. For the moment, let's not waste any time guessing what's what. We should simply follow Shoonik. He knows exactly what he's doing. I truly trust his instincts, and I am sure that he is headed toward the right direction."

"I agree. Let's just follow him."

They covered fifty kilometers leisurely within fifteen minutes and arrived at the French border. Uncle and niece were exuberantly happy to have succeeded in getting to France. To demonstrate their appreciation, they patted Shoonik on the head. Indeed, both were thankful for having the best guide on Planet Heaven.

At the French frontier, a long glass wall extended between two tall columns of sparkling marble, marking the border. As they approached it, the glass partition suddenly slid open in a smooth rhythmic fashion. Two polite and smiling French guards in blue uniforms stood tall behind a white marble platform. They instantly waved the dog, Martha, and her uncle into France, without asking any questions.

Martha was filled with a feeling of awe. Planet Heaven was really majestic! Its France was as superbly beautiful as the one on Earth. Martha always called the earthly France magical.

Turning to one of the friendly guards, Martha asked in fluent French, "How can we find Georges Bizet in Paris?" She hesitated a second, then added, "This is Paris, isn't it?"

Sooren hearing her niece's question, gave her a crooked smile. Martha immediately realized the reason for that meaningful smile. She remembered him telling her that she should trust her pet's instincts. Why was she then doubting him?

"Yes, it is," he responded. "To find an address in Paris, you have to go way down from here to rue Vaughirard, where you will come across the tourist bureau. Once there, ask the clerk. He or she will help you with Bizet's exact address."

The guard who had been speaking with Sooren and Martha, turned to his colleague and said, "You know Bizet? The same composer who has composed the famous opera *Carmen.*"

He nodded. "Yes, of course I know him. But, it is strange. Nobody talks about him nowadays. We never hear his music on any radio station."

Martha sighed and shook her head. *How can people forget about such a famous composer? Even Jesus, who had not thought about Bizet before I talked with him about the composer.*

The trajectory to the tourist bureau was swift. Thanks to Shoonik, who knew some shortcuts, they found themselves standing in front of a two-story green building within seconds. It resembled a Swiss chalet with its shingled façade and several pots of lilac, lilies, and geraniums decorating the windows.

Martha stepped into the bright, shining office, followed by her uncle and Shoonik, and walked straight to the clerk.

"Hi, how can I help you?" asked a young woman dressed in white, with a dark complexion and brown hair.

"I'm looking for Georges Bizet."

"The nineteenth-century composer?"

"Yes, madam," Martha answered.

"Let me see," the clerk said, peering at her computer. She began clicking away at different links, as she opened one site after another.

"Oh! Here—I've got it!" she finally said.

"How exciting! I can't wait to find him!" Martha exclaimed.

The clerk sized up Martha, not understanding her enthusiasm. "Georges Bizet lives at a boarding house called Chez Escudier."

"Could you kindly give me the exact address?" Martha asked.

"One second," she said as she reexamined the specific site on the computer. The clerk pulled out a small pad from her drawer and wrote: "Rive Gauche, Avenue Pascal number fifteen."

Martha grabbed the piece of paper with the address eagerly, thanked the clerk, and dashed out to inform her uncle and Shoonik of Georges Bizet's precise location. Being tired of waiting, they had moved out into the street.

"I had no idea Paris would be such a spectacular city," Sooren said, as they walked on the beautiful, broad Avenue des Champs-Élysées with its rows of clipped chestnut trees stretching all along the far-reaching boulevard. The Champs-Élysées ran for 1.9 km and ended at the Arc de Triomphe. The elaborate arch honors those who fought for France, especially during the Napoleonic Wars.

On Earth, the Champs-Élysées is known for its different monuments, active outdoor and indoor cafés, and high-fashion designer stores. It is known as one of the most magnificent streets in the world. To Martha, it seemed exactly the same on Planet Heaven.

Martha looked around her with admiration. "Paris is unique in its charm and beauty," she told her uncle. "When I was alive, after we had moved to the States, Americans wanted to know about my favorite place among all the countries that we had lived in or visited. I told them that undoubtedly, it was Paris."

"And I guess you visited Paris with Zaven several times during those days, didn't you?"

Martha sighed and looked away to hide her tears from her uncle. She was sure that Sooren was by then fed up with her teary eyes each time that Zaven's name was mentioned.

Presently, Martha brushed a strand of hair away from her face and murmured absently, "Of course, many…many times." Then, staring far out toward the *Arc de Triomphe*, she added, "Oh, Uncle, you already know that every time that we speak of my darling husband, I wish he were here with me."

Sooren nodded. "I understand. But don't keep talking about this subject so much. Let the man enjoy a bit more time on Earth with his children and grandchildren."

"I can't help it. He was my best friend. But you're right. I should leave the poor man alone. Besides, our family members have the right to have Zaven with them for as long as they can."

"That's my girl!" Sooren said, and patted Martha on the shoulder.

As they walked up the Champs-Élysées, cars zoomed by and honked their horns incessantly, just like the Parisians did on Earth. Martha reminded herself that people of different nationalities always remain the same in certain ways, even on Planet Heaven.

While still strolling along the breathtakingly beautiful Champs-Élysées, Martha noticed a teenager who looked exactly like Haroot, her son, when he was about the same age.

Chapter 42

Haroot

Back on Earth in the mid-1980s, when Haroot was just fourteen and Sylvia was seventeen, Martha and her family lived in Monnetier, France. Haroot was a good-looking teenager back then and resembled the French actor Alain Delon, with his green eyes, light-brown hair, and pale complexion. Martha had enjoyed her son's company very much. Indeed, mother and son were good chums. They even sometimes did crazy things together, such as crashing against their unfriendly neighbor's wall—of course, accidentally—while they were riding a motorcycle. The same was true concerning Martha's relationship with Sylvia, with whom she drove across central France and had a fun vacation.

Martha was trying in vain to detach herself from her husband, children, and family members. Meanwhile, she was well aware that her behavior was somewhat bothersome to Uncle Sooren. He already had heard too much about everything concerning Martha's past. Despite all that, she could not control herself. Today, having seen that young fellow who looked like Haroot, it was impossible for her to remain silent.

"Uncle Sooren," Martha said, "look at that teenager chatting with the other chap a few feet away."

"Yes, what about him?"

"Uncle, he looks so much like Haroot."

"Oh, not again!"

"Uncle, I promise you. You'll love this story."

"I will?" he uttered, roaring with laughter. "What's new?"

"No, uncle, I mean it. He looks exactly like Haroot when he was a teenager when we lived in Monnetier-Mornex."

"You're talking about the chap standing by that store?"

"Yes, Uncle. Honestly, he is the copy of the teenager Haroot. It is just like an apple cut in half," she said, sounding very excited. "Can I tell you a story concerning Haroot during the days when we were living in France, and he was going to a school tucked away in the mountainous region of Regnier?"

"Yeah, go right ahead. I can tell that you are dying to share the story with me."

Martha did not waste a minute. "Haroot hated the high school there."

She recounted that her son kept complaining about the students and saying they were all peasants and stank of cow manure.

"Honestly, Mom. They stink so badly that I have to hold my breath," he'd say.

Thinking that Haroot was a spoiled child, she chided him. Then one night, Martha had to attend a parents' meeting at the school.

"Uncle, you know what? After that day, I realized that Haroot's complaint was not based on his being spoiled. He was right. Even the parents stank of cow manure." Martha laughed her head off as Sooren joined her. "That night at Haroot's school, if I were not embarrassed, I would have held a handkerchief to my nose. The parents really smelled horribly."

Another time, Martha added, she was supposed to fetch Haroot from school to drive him to his doctor for an afternoon appointment.

"The day of the doctor's visit, Haroot asked his teacher's permission to leave class an hour before the school closing, to meet me by the school entrance."

Martha had been exhausted from running errands all morning, so she decided to take a short nap. She had been absolutely sure that she would wake up on time for her rendezvous with Haroot.

"Unfortunately, I overslept by fifteen minutes."

"Goodness, what happened? Did Haroot miss his doctor's appointment?"

"I woke up with a start and rushed to the school. Haroot told me that he didn't mind at all waiting for me. The problem was he got into trouble with the school principal."

Haroot explained that while he was waiting for her by the school entrance, the principal had passed by several times and looked at him suspiciously. At one point, he had approached Haroot and asked what business he had standing by the school gate during class hours.

He had answered he had a doctor's appointment and added that his mother was supposed to pick him up. "I hope you are telling the truth, and this is not a convenient lie to help you get away from class," the principal had told Haroot.

Annoyed with the principal for not trusting him, Haroot had answered him in an angry tone of voice, "I don't need to lie to you. If I wish to get out of your boring school, I will just walk out."

Chapter 43

Defiance

"Very interesting. I'm sure the principal punished Haroot," Sooren commented.

Martha bit her lip. "I was really sorry to have created such an awkward situation for my child, especially because I found the punishment to be stupid and demeaning."

The principal had ordered Haroot to write two hundred times: *When Mr. Principal speaks to me, I will answer politely.*

"Oh my God! That's such a primitive idea of a punishment."

"I know," Martha said. "That's why I forbade Haroot from obeying the principal."

The following day, the principal summoned Martha to his office.

"Madam, your son told me that you didn't allow him to carry out the punishment I'd assigned him. I'm really shocked at you."

Martha said she had looked down at her feet, feeling somewhat uneasy, and answered, "Sir, I think that kind of a punishment is very humiliating for a boy of fourteen. It is childish and primitive."

"Excuse me!" the principal had exclaimed. "All the children respect and obey my orders, but your son...Now I see why. He has an arrogant mother like you!"

"Is that so?" Martha had said sarcastically. "Maybe, but you know what, sir? If you had given him a broom, mop, and a bucket full of water, and asked him to sweep and wash your whole school, I would have supported you one hundred percent. But not for an ancient-style six-year-old child's punishment."

The principal shook his head and sighed. He probably told himself that it was no use. He was wasting his time.

Chapter 44

Escudier

As Martha was telling the story of Haroot's punishment, Shoonik interrupted her by hopping up and down on his hind legs. He seemed to be trying to sniff the piece of paper with Bizet's address written on it, which Martha held in her hand.

Sooren, observing Shoonik's behavior, laughed heartily. He told Martha, "Yeah, who else better than your favorite pet to lead us to Bizet?"

Martha agreed, bobbing her head. She was really proud of her lovely Shoonik. What's more, Martha believed that she was blessed to have an uncle such as Sooren who took her mission in finding the famous French composer as seriously as Martha herself. Yes, she was indeed very lucky for Sooren, her heavenly companion. In fact, she couldn't have asked for any better and more loving pals such as Sooren and her loyal and devoted pet. Both of them took their mission to help Martha seriously. What's more, she was extremely fortunate that her dog's instincts were so accurate. Although Uncle Sooren was able to find his way through the help of his iPhone, Shoonik could figure out the correct direction and location simply by sniffing the piece of paper with Bizet's address.

Shoonik began scurrying on the Champs-Élysées with Martha and Sooren closely following at his heels. Before reaching the Arc de Triomphe, they turned into a side street where the famous Le Relais de l'Entrecôte restaurant was located. In Paris on Earth, the same restaurant serves only steak and fries. On Planet Heaven, however, nobody ate meat. Animals were not slaughtered for food the way they were on Earth. Martha was very curious to find out what they served at the heavenly Le Relais de l'Entrecôte.

"Here, they must serve fries and delicious tofu steaks," Sooren said. "Would you like to have lunch now at Le Relais de l'Entrecôte? I'll invite you."

"No, thanks. I'm not that hungry. Besides, I'm very eager to find Bizet first. We can always eat later."

"Are you sure? I promise you that tofu looks and tastes exactly like meat."

"I know, but I'm one hundred percent sure that I don't want to eat right now. How about you?"

"No, I'm fine."

So, they continued crossing the winding, narrow road where Le Relais de l'Entrecôte was located. Martha noticed myriad outdoor cafés and designer-clothing shops bustling with people. Like in earthly France, beautiful, elegantly dressed women sat reading their newspapers and drinking coffee in the cafés with their dogs lying on the floor next to them.

At the end of the street, they turned to the right and went a long distance before reaching Palais de Chaillot where, from a high platform, they could see the majestic Tour d'Eiffel stretching its imposing tower high up into the sky. On the platform, looking down toward Tour d'Eiffel, there were two groups of musicians and a hip-hop dancer performing merrily. The two visitors with Shoonik on their side, stood around for a while and watched the performers with great interest. Martha and Uncle Sooren even moved their hips to the tune of the rap music.

Shoonik began panting with his red tongue hanging out from the side of his mouth; as his jet-black coat glowed brightly. Martha, who had always liked German shepherd dogs, looked at him admiringly. "My handsome Shoonik," she called out. "Are you tired, baby? Do you want to rest a bit?"

Shoonik instead urged on, looking even more resolute than before.

"Martha," Sooren said, "I think we are getting closer to our destination. I can tell from Shoonik's behavior."

Soon, they arrived at the shady, tree-lined, private-looking Avenue Molière. Shoonik stopped in front of a wrought-iron gate at the end of the street, where some green jasmine branches from high bushes passed over the top of the closed gate. The pleasant aroma of those beautiful white flowers permeated the air.

A gray plaque with Escudier carved on it in white letters hung on the wall, by the gate.

"This is it, Uncle Sooren!" Martha giggled, looking radiantly happy. Yes, she finally had achieved her mission, thanks to the support and help of Uncle Sooren and Shoonik.

Uncle Sooren scratched his head and said, "Martha, please remind me of who Escudier is."

"Léon Escudier," Martha began to explain, "is the same critic who in 1875, after the first performance of *Carmen*, wrote a nasty critique in his newspaper the following morning."

"Oh yes. I remember now."

Chapter 45

Carmen

Bizet's opera *Carmen* did not fit into the special framework of the traditional opéra comique of 1874 France. It was a real revolutionary work that shocked other musicians and critics.

Bizet finished the score for the innovative opera during the summer. His new creation premiered on March 3, 1875. That day, present in the audience were some renowned musicians, such as Jules Massenet, Camille Saint-Saëns, and Charles Gounod. The first two composers were congratulatory, but Charles Gounod was quite hostile to Bizet and accused Bizet of plagiarism. Furthermore, much of the press comment was negative. One specific journalist who was harsher than the rest happened to be Escudier, the same character in whose boarding house Bizet now resided.

Carmen, the heroine in the opera, is a fiery and seductive young woman who drives men crazy by her amorous and enticing behavior. Unlike other operatic stories, she is not the pious type, supposed to endure pain and suffering for the sake of her love. She is devilish and impish.

The musical composition of *Carmen* was totally revolutionary for a nineteenth-century culture. In a way, one can claim that Bizet helped revolutionize the style and composition of scores in opera by this lively and daring piece of work. He brought an animated mood and style into the world of the opera. The flamenco music of *Carmen* made the audience stamp their feet joyously and sway their bodies rhythmically to the lively tempo.

Martha thought that not only did Bizet introduce a unique musical chef d'oeuvre, but he also stirred the lives of other leading musical figures of the time. Unfortunately, his daring action was quite risky for him. It was just like digging his own grave or hanging himself. Yes, he rocked the boat and disturbed the emotional frame of mind of certain figures. In turn, those people shattered him and his hopes. They broke his heart and prompted his early death. The poor Bizet died at the young age of thirty-six. The performance the night that he passed away was cancelled; performances of *Carmen* resumed later that year. The irony is that at that point, the press that had condemned his work previously exploded with positive reviews and approbation. They called Bizet "a real master." Yes, the same media that had condemned his work months earlier now praised him, except for Escudier. How unfair!

Chapter 46

Martha's Plan

Martha always had sympathized with Bizet because she had felt similar disappointment when certain publishers and agents had unfairly shattered her hopes.

During such episodes, Martha had remained miserable and sad for weeks on end. She began thinking that she was wasting her time and that she was not a good writer. But after a while, life would become normal again, and Martha's desire for having her books published would continue. Ultimately, she was not the kind of person who would be defeated by any negative response from the agents.

That's why Martha persevered in finding her favorite musician on Planet Heaven. She wished to bring a message of hope to Bizet by informing him of his great fame on Earth after his death. Martha was certain that Georges Bizet did not have any inkling about his postmortem popularity. Martha also wished to relay to Bizet that she, of all the people, was well aware how heartbreaking it was to be judged harshly for a work that he himself thought was a masterpiece. However, besides intending to relay the good news to Bizet, Martha just wanted to meet her favorite musician in person.

Chapter 47

A Notification

As Martha, Sooren, and Shoonik reached Bizet's address, Sooren's iPhone beeped, indicating the receipt of an e-mail. He immediately, opened the e-mail and read:

An important notification—
 This is to inform Martha that Zaven will be arriving sometime within a year. He will be staying at Martha's family's residence. His mother will also join him.

Martha's heart skipped a beat with joy. Was it true? Was she really going to see Zaven so soon? *That should mean good news to Sooren*, she mused. From this day forward, he does not have to listen to stories about her husband. In the meantime, Martha became even more resolute to go ahead with her mission. She told herself, *I would like to hurry up and see Georges Bizet. Then I can return home to prepare things properly for Zaven's arrival.*

"Do you want to return to Iran, to get ready for Zaven's arrival to Planet Heaven?" Uncle Sooren asked Martha. "We could always come back at a later date, now that we know where Bizet lives. Really, I mean it. We can easily come back. We could even bring Zaven along."

"No, not at all! I'm confident that we will accomplish our goal way before Zaven's arrival. Besides, knowing Zaven, I vouch that he will have lots of projects to attend to the moment he gets here."

Sooren beamed cheerfully and stared at her niece with pride. He seemed to be approving of Martha's attitude toward life on Planet Heaven.

Martha's eyes shone like hundred-volt light bulbs. She smiled with satisfaction and thought that her enthusiasm and willpower were even stronger than before. She was absolutely certain about her intentions. Yes, nothing could now dissuade Martha from her goal concerning meeting the musician in person. The only sore point bothering her slightly was that for some unknown reason she was starting to feel a bit apprehensive. She wondered if there was some danger lurking in the air.

"Isn't this supposed to be Planet Heaven?" Martha asked. "Shouldn't there be nothing but goodness existing on this planet?"

"Yes, you are right to think the way you do. However, very rarely, evil hides itself among the good."

"Really? I thought Heaven was Heaven. Back on Earth, some people believe that hell exists, which is supposed to belong to the Prince of Darkness."

"True, and evil should only prevail in hell and not here on our sacred planet," Sooren said. He stared far into the distance as some Parisians strolled leisurely by.

"It is much more complicated than we can comprehend," he continued. "All I know is that God grants free will to people not only on Earth, but also on Planet Heaven."

Martha rubbed her cheek with contemplation. "I wonder how God deals with evil up here."

"All I know is that He gives them a chance to repent of their ways. If they do, then they abide a peaceful life, like the rest of us."

"And what if they don't?"

"In that case, they'll be sent to the Reform Center."

Chapter 48

Mission Accomplished

Martha pressed the doorbell with both great dread and excitement. She was happy to have found Bizet so speedily. It had hardly been a week since her arrival to Planet Heaven. Indeed, she was really thrilled and could not wait to lay her eyes upon the great musician.

Martha asked herself, *I wonder how he looks. The same as in his earthly pictures?*

Well, never mind, Martha thought. She reminded herself that the most important issue was the fact that she was presently standing upon the doorstep of Bizet's residence. Martha couldn't believe her good luck. *If only my family back on Earth knew about my adventurous life on Planet Heaven!*

"The main building must be some distance from the gate. That's why it's taking them so long to open the door," Martha said, beaming.

The moment she said those words, they heard some movement taking place behind the door. "Who is it?" a thick, manly voice echoed.

Martha did not give Sooren a chance to answer and interjected, "My name's Martha. I'm here with Mr. Sooren Nahapetian to visit Mr. Georges Bizet."

Silence. Martha's loud heartbeat resonated in her head, just like the sort of drumming one hears in jazz compositions.

"Hello? Would you open the door, please?" Martha called out impatiently.

Sooren marveled at Martha's brave character. He himself began feeling slightly suspicious of the mysterious atmosphere lingering in the air. Shoonik, meanwhile, began whining loudly as Martha patted his head, trying to reassure him that things were all right.

Soon, they both heard the exchange of some conversation going on between the person behind the door and another voice spilling out of a walkie-talkie. Then Martha and Sooren heard an additional exchange of words between the same characters—maybe the doorkeeper or an armed guard and the voice.

"There are some people behind the door asking to visit Georges Bizet. Can I let them in?" the man asked.

There was some unintelligible mumbling from the walkie-talkie, and within seconds, the door rolled open with a loud squeak.

"Ouch, my ears!" Martha complained. "This gate badly needs to be greased."

Martha and Sooren were surprised to see two black-uniformed, unfriendly guards with thick mustaches. The guards clung firmly to their machine guns.

"Wow, take it easy! We are not here to declare war on you. On the contrary, we are visiting you on a friendly mission," Martha declared.

The two guards were in no mood for such talk. They immediately thrust the two in front of them, pressing their guns into their backs. Meanwhile, Shoonik suddenly disappeared into thin air.

Chapter 49

As Brave as Ever

The hostile guards shoved Sooren and Martha through a picturesque garden crowded by cypress, birch, pine, and spruce trees. In spite of the threatening situation, Martha could not ignore the beauty of the vast yard. She noted green bushes with red, white, and yellow flowers fanning out their branches like stretched arms.

As the two fierce sentinels brutally pushed them onward through the paved path that coiled through the yard, Sooren muttered under his breath, "I had no idea we had such nasty thugs living in our Heaven. If I'd known, I wouldn't have allowed you to set out on such a dangerous expedition."

Martha did not answer. She was busy wondering about Shoonik's absence. Where was he? Was Shoonik hiding from the evil guards, or did he have a special scheme in mind? She did not wish to bring it to her uncle's attention. *Whatever he is up to*, she told herself, *I am sure it is noble.* Martha smiled, her heart overflowing with love for Shoonik. *I know my dog and trust him. This is the precious, lovely pet of mine that on Earth*

protected me against evildoers. How about those nasty Persian boys?
The same ones who chased me and sang offensive rhymes. Yes, just
because I was a little Christian girl. The same ones who called me
spiritually unclean. Shoonik never left me alone after my father's
death. I always counted on him to look after me.

One guard now shoved his rifle harder against Martha's
back and sneered, "Hey, old lady, why aren't you afraid? I
would think you'd be shivering with fear by now."

As the two ruffians roared with laughter, Martha responded, "Afraid? Of you hooligans? Of course I'm not afraid, you
fool! What do you think you can do, kill me?"

"Yes, of course! Are you blind? Can't you see my powerful
machine gun?"

"Yes, I can see your mighty gun, my friend! Don't you see
how I'm trembling with fear?" Martha uttered with a sarcastic tone of voice. Then she gave the guard a nasty look and
continued, "Go ahead. Kill me if you can."

"Of course I can," he said, creasing his brow.

"I've already died once, stupid! I don't think you can do
much to harm me anymore."

Both guards remained silent, and Sooren began laughing. He remembered how bold Martha had always been, even
as a teenager. In Iran, when fundamentalist men sometimes
tried to molest women who were not covered up under hijabs,
Martha was never afraid to confront them.

Once, when Zaven, Martha, and the children had returned to Iran for a short period of time, the TV and newspapers announced that certain taxi drivers had kidnapped
women, raped them, and killed them.

Hearing this horrible news, Zaven told Martha, "If ever
a taxi driver drives you off trying to harm you, I want you to

keep calm. When you see that he is trying to make advances, kick him in the groin!"

"Got it. No worries; I know exactly how to do it," Martha said confidently.

Ironically, Martha did undergo such an experience. After having returned from Germany and having lived in Iran for only one year, Zaven was once again transferred to a foreign country. In fact, he found a job with a major American company, working as marketing manager in Geneva. At the time, Martha was twenty-seven and a good-looking woman. Since they were supposed to leave Tehran the following day, Martha's sister-in-law Lionel—the wife of her brother Artash—invited them for lunch. Martha needed to run some errands that day, so she asked Zaven to take the kids to her brother's house. She explained that as soon as she completed her errands, she would join them there.

Chapter 50

Kidnapping Attempt

In Tehran, a taxicab could give a ride to several passengers heading toward a common direction. That day, when Martha waved down a cab already occupied by two other passengers, the driver stopped and picked her up. Martha's destination was supposed to be the next stop. However, when they arrived at the designated location, the taxi driver simply drove on.

Martha protested, "Hey, mister, you passed my stop!"

"Did I?" he said casually. "That's too bad! Sorry, I completely forgot. Let me drop off these two passengers, and then I'll bring you back to your stop."

As they drove on, the driver delivered the other two passengers to their drop-off points. But he did not turn around to deliver Martha back to her stop. He sped like mad toward a desolate area, staring at Martha continually through the rearview mirror.

Martha did not know what to think. "I don't recognize these streets. Are you taking the long way to make me pay more?"

The guy snorted and did not respond.

"I promise you that I will not pay a penny more than what we had agreed upon when you picked me up on that street."

He sniggered again, shaking his head. "Who said I am taking you to your destination?"

"Excuse me?"

This time, he laughed loudly.

OK, Martha thought. *If that's what you want, I know how to handle a fool like you!*

The obnoxious driver asked, "Aren't you afraid that I might kidnap you? Haven't you heard the most recent news?"

"No, I am not afraid at all!" Martha said.

Martha had hardly uttered those words, when the driver had turned around and sped toward the spot where she was supposed to be dropped off. Martha could not understand the reason for the fellow's change of heart. Was it because she had stayed calm and brave? The driver had probably wished to have some fun scaring his female passenger; especially that the news of the kidnappings was the hot topic of the day. However, if his intentions were to scare Martha, he must have realized that he was dealing with the wrong person.

Chapter 51

Escudier—The Real Scoundrel

The guards led Sooren and Martha up a set of four steps into a hotel lobby, where women guests meandered, dressed in fashionable outfits, such as 1920s-style round hats with narrow brims and long maxi coats. Men wore double-breasted and vested suits with beige or brown caps. The old-fashioned outfits may have looked outdated on Earth, but up here, they looked very appropriate and complemented the surroundings.

For some reason, the guests seemed too preoccupied in order to notice Martha and her uncle being accompanied by two rough armed guards. With drinks in hand, they were busy chattering, laughing, and having a great time. *Could it be that they were used to seeing such scenes*, Martha wondered, *or were they blind?*

At the reception desk, a tall attendant wearing a black vest and white button-down shirt brushed his hand against his wavy dark hair. Wearing a broad, artificial smile, he asked Martha and Sooren, "How can I help you?"

Martha turned to Uncle Sooren and murmured, "How can he talk to us with a smile on his face when he sees these guards pressing their guns against our backs?"

"I know. I can't understand it, either!"

"By the way," the receptionist said casually, "My name is Escudier. I am the proprietor of the hotel."

"Oh. Yes, I thought you would be Escudier," Martha said.

"How do you know about me?" Escudier asked, furrowing his brow.

Martha smiled mischievously and answered, "I read about you when I was still alive. Anyway, never mind about how I know about you. We are here to visit Georges Bizet. Could you point us to his room?"

"His room…Oh yes, his room." Escudier laughed heartily, with tears running down his cheeks. "Guards, guide them to Bizet's *room*."

The guards escorted them around the corner and down the corridor to a set of long steps. At the bottom of the staircase, they saw a black, heavy door, which the guards unlocked. The door opened with a loud groan, exposing a dark vault. The two armed men shoved Sooren and Martha into the somber crypt.

They walked cautiously in the dark, clearing the way of some cobwebs, which brushed against their faces. Then, gradually, as their eyes grew accustomed to the dusky environment, they saw cells with iron-grilled doors toward the end of the dungeon.

Chapter 52

A Dream Come True

Martha and Sooren rubbed their eyes to make sure the situation they were facing was real and not the outcome of their imaginations. As they stood dumbfounded by the cells, one of the unfriendly guards thrust them violently into one of the prison cubicles.

"What?" Martha protested. "You mean you are going to lock us up as your prisoners?"

"No, dear madam. We are going to give you a luxurious suite in the main boardinghouse building!" he said, roaring with laughter.

Martha sighed and said, "Honestly! This is not heard of on Planet Heaven. You guys must be savages."

The guard grew angry at Martha's arrogance. "You silly woman! If you don't shut up, I will shove my gun into your mouth."

Martha ignored the nasty fellow and said, "At least tell us what we have done wrong."

Sooren yelled at the guard, "Hey, man, can't you talk nicely? Honestly, I had no idea this kind of evil place existed on Planet Heaven. It is worse than on Earth!"

"Now you know," the second guard said. "Besides, you dumb people, you want to know what stupid thing you have done? You have found Bizet. That's what you're not supposed to do!"

The first guard cut in, bobbing his head, wearing a sarcastic smirk. "Exactly. My colleague is right. Did you have to come here and disturb our peace?"

Uncle Sooren shook his head with disappointment. "It seems that nobody taught you any manners. That's no way to talk to a lady."

"Lady!" the brute answered mockingly. "No real lady would travel all this way to meet a tramp like Bizet."

"Listen, guard," Uncle Sooren said. "Why don't you keep me here and let my niece go free?"

"You're joking, right?" he sneered, pointing his gun at him.

"No, I'm not joking. Just set her free."

"No, no, Uncle Sooren. I don't want to go."

The guard locked the cell door and marched away without further discussion. He then slammed the basement door behind him with a loud bang.

When Martha's eyes slowly adjusted to the dark subterranean vault, she noticed a few other cage like stalls across the basement walls. The cells were vacant, except for the one beside theirs. Gradually, the form of a man with matted long hair came into view. The prisoner's head was bent over some sheet music. It looked like he was busy composing a song or a musical score.

Noticing the presence of some companions in the next cell, the unkempt inmate turned to them and waved amicably through the bars.

"Who are you two? What are your names?" he asked in a husky voice.

Martha introduced her uncle and herself to the prisoner. Staring intensely into the darkness of the basement at the mysterious fellow, she questioned hesitantly, "You wouldn't by any chance be Georges Bizet, would you?"

Before the fellow had a chance to reply, Sooren whispered into her ear, "Why don't you give the guy a chance to introduce himself when he feels like it?"

Martha did not answer. Instead she made an effort to remember Bizet's appearance based on some pictures she had seen of him back on Earth.

"Why do you want to know?" the man demanded.

"Well, from the moment I've set foot on Planet Heaven, I've been determined to find Georges Bizet. I wish to give him some good news," Martha said.

The prisoner, who had not stopped working on his sheet music, suddenly raised his head. He pushed back a bunch of matted hair from his forehead and tried to make out who this woman was. Then, squinting his eyes a few times, he said, "Well, whoever you are, madam—by the way, what did you say, your names were?"

"My name is Martha. Martha Davidian. I'm one of your musical fans. This is my uncle, Sooren."

He gazed at them absently and asked, "OK, tell me about the good news."

Martha let out a shrill cry and uttered, "Uncle Sooren, I was right. It is indeed Georges Bizet!"

As Martha began recounting George Bizet's fame on Earth after his death, Sooren cut in. "I can't believe it! Mr. Bizet, why have they imprisoned you?"

Bizet seemed to be pleased to hear about his enduring fame on Earth. "Well, it's a long story," he answered. "For some reason, Mr. Escudier does not seem to like me very much. However, despite all that, he orders me to compose some music for him each day."

Martha reminded herself that Escudier, who founded the journal *L'Art musical* on Earth when still alive, was totally against Bizet. He had called *Carmen*'s music "dull and obscure" in his review. He went on to say, "The ear grows weary of waiting for the cadence that never comes."

He also declared that Bizet had plagiarized Gounod's work while, in reality, none of Bizet's works resembled those of Gounod. *Carmen* was unique in its style of composition. Gounod and Escudier also called *Carmen*'s musical structure "immoral." Why then accuse Bizet of plagiarism? Did it mean that Gounod's style was also immoral?

Sooren asked Bizet, "What will happen if you refuse to compose for him?"

"Why should I refuse? If I don't write, I'll rot in this lousy and musty prison."

Martha in her heart agreed with Bizet. How else could one pass the time in that rotten dungeon? Meanwhile, she wondered what Escudier did with Bizet's music on Planet Heaven.

Georges Bizet began coughing harshly. When Martha asked him if he was ill, he answered, "What do you expect? Having lived in this dark and humid dungeon, without being exposed to any sun rays at all for centuries, do you think anybody in my place would feel healthy?"

Martha and Sooren shook their heads. Seeing their sad expressions, Bizet said, "Let us not despair. Yes, let's say everything's all right to make life bearable in this dreary prison. OK?"

Martha, thinking about Bizet's optimistic tone, said, "I am sure you haven't read any of Ella Wheeler Wilcox's poems."

"No, what about her?"

Instead of answering Bizet, Martha began reciting some relevant verses:

Talk health. The dreary, never-ending tale
Of mortal maladies is worn and stale;
You cannot charm or interest or please
By harping on that minor chord, disease.
So, say that you are well and all is well with you,
And God shall hear your words and make them true.

Bizet smiled and sighed with relief. "What matters now is that I have some companions! Can you imagine what I have gone through all this time?"

Martha jumped to her feet and said, "Oh God, why would anybody try to imprison such an important and harmless person?"

Sooren whispered in Martha's ear, "Escudier and Gounod, being jealous of him, probably don't want him to get well known on Planet Heaven."

"They don't want anybody to know that I'm here. Gounod must be using my work to add to his own collection. I'm sure that he must be pretending that they are his musical compositions. Not bad, eh?"

Bizet continued to explain that he thought that if he refused to write for them, they would never let him out of that prison. Of course, he knew quite well that if he dared to be defiant, they would make him suffer even more.

Chapter 53

The Atmosphere in the Dark, Cold Cell

It could well have been months since Martha and Sooren had been locked up in Escudier's prison cell. They had completely lost track of time. They did try to ask the hostile guards when they delivered their daily meager meals, but the guards merely roared with laughter. Strangely enough, despite everything, neither Sooren nor Martha felt depressed or unhappy.

The reason was because of Bizet. They enjoyed the company of their cellmate so immensely that both were convinced they could stay there with him forever. True, he did not socialize the way other people on Earth would. However, thanks to him, Martha and Soren learned to immerse themselves into a deeper and richer style of music. It was totally different from what they knew.

Martha wondered if the jail conditions had anything to do with Bizet's current musical style. Whatever the cause,

Martha thought that the composer's behavior filled the dark surroundings with brightness. Whenever he composed his heavenly compositions, Martha and Sooren could feel music in the air despite the lack of musical instruments. Yes, Georges Bizet made the atmosphere vibrate with life as he composed and sang.

In Sooren's and Martha's minds, their prison atmosphere was filled with an unexplainable mystical rhythm. Indeed, every moment of the day for them was chock-full of mysterious melodies. Therefore, the humid and cavernous cell transformed itself into a luminous habitat. Meanwhile, the guards took turns walking into the jail twice a day, throwing a few scraps of bread and some cheese at them for their breakfast, lunch, and dinner.

Chapter 54

Mao, Mei, and Sandy

One day, Bizet said to Martha and Sooren, "I have never asked you how you two managed to find me."

Martha said, "My dog, Shoonik, helped us find you."

Bizet arched his eyebrows. "Come on. Be serious!"

"Yes, sir! I promise you that I am telling you the truth." She giggled, held her head up proudly, and continued. "My dog is a clever son of a dog!"

Bizet laughed. "Tell me how he helped you to find me."

Remembering her loyal Shoonik, Martha felt a slight pain in her heart. She sighed and answered, "Well, Shoonik is an old-timer on Planet Heaven and knows his way around."

Bizet nodded. "I see."

Martha told Bizet about how they first had found his address, then the manner in which Shoonik had led them to Escudier's boarding house. She went on to explain everything about her beloved dog.

"It looks like you are an animal lover. I'm sure that you had many other pets in your life other than Shoonik," Bizet said.

"Yes, all through my life I've had nice cats and dogs, but no rodents, snakes, or any turtles," Martha said, laughing loudly. She remembered them one by one while her mind wandered into her past life on Earth.

"Why don't you talk to me about the ones that you really liked?" Bizet insisted. "It would be a good way of killing time."

Sooren laughed and said, "Yes, what else do we have to do in this cursed den? Let's talk."

Martha did not have to think long.

"I loved all my pets. Each one had a special place in my heart. I must stress that I never regarded them as my pets but my family members."

Martha told them how Shoonik had been the best childhood companion of her life, especially after her father's passing.

"The day I learned I had to say good-bye to my lovely Shoonik was the worst day in my life. Every time I remember that separation, I can't help but cry."

"What happened? Why did you have to separate from him?" Bizet asked compassionately. Martha sensed that Bizet had begun to feel a kinship with her and Sooren. A strong bond was developing among the three of them.

To answer Bizet's question, Martha told him about the reason why she had to separate from Shoonik after her father's death.

Martha scanned the dark and vacant dungeon with melancholic eyes and sighed. The gloomy atmosphere of the cellar didn't do any good to her sad memory of the day she threw her arms around Shoonik's neck and cried bitterly. They had had no choice. They were moving to Tehran from Arak, and the landlord in Tehran absolutely had forbidden them from bringing in any pets into their newly rented home.

"Who took your dog?" Bizet asked.

"A village owner who appeared to be a nice person said he needed a dog like Shoonik to roam about in their vast land and protect them and their property."

After Martha and her family moved to Tehran, she received a letter from a friend, saying Shoonik had returned by himself all the way from the remote village and was lingering about their old house in Arak.

Martha wiped her tears and swallowed the lump in her throat. "I wish Shoonik could talk and tell me what happened after he returned from the faraway village. Did he die right away? Did the owner of our previous house take him in?"

"Never mind," Uncle Sooren said, draping an arm around Martha's shoulder. "The main thing is that you found him on Planet Heaven."

"Yes, you are right. Besides, I am sure that we will see him soon."

Bizet replied, "Do you think so? Do you really think we'll get relieved out of this hellish situation?"

"I hope so!" Martha said. She decided to talk about Mei, her family's small Abyssinian cat, and then their pedigreed European tiger cat, Mao. They had acquired Mao in Geneva, where they had lived for ten years. Together with their cairn terrier, Sandy, Mao was a well-traveled cat. He had lived with the family in Switzerland, Iran, England, France, Spain, and the United States.

Chapter 55

Some Funny Incidents

Martha suddenly remembered what Georges Bizet had asked her, and uttered, "Oh yes. You asked me to recount some funny incidents about my pets. Two stories come to mind. One is about Mei."

Martha told them that Mei, their small-built Abyssinian cat who had a long, straight tail sticking up in the air, was indeed a clever creature. Haroot had found her in a tree in their garden when they were living in Tehran.

One day, Zaven was cooking in the kitchen. He took out a stack of hamburgers from the refrigerator and placed them on the countertop. He turned around to fetch the skillet and the oil to start preparing the burgers, but when he returned, the stack of hamburgers had disappeared.

"Where did you put my hamburgers?" he asked Martha.

"I did not touch them," Martha protested.

"Yes, you did. There is nobody here but you and me."

"I promise you that I did not touch them."

"Are you playing some kind of a trick on me?" Zaven barked.

They kept arguing while Mei sat innocently in a corner.

The following morning, when Soghra, their maid was cleaning the kitchen, she removed the grill in front of the fridge to clean under the refrigerator. As she reached the long-handled broom underneath the fridge, she pulled out the stack of hamburgers, a big piece of cooked chicken, and a chunk of barbecued meat. Martha now could understand the reason for the foul smell in the kitchen for the past two days.

Martha said that she had looked at Mei, who always sat in the kitchen, and said, "You mischievous devil. Now I know who stole the hamburgers. I think you know quite well that you made me and Zaven fight like two mad dogs over those hamburgers, don't you?"

Sooren and Bizet laughed heartily. Bizet said, "That naughty little cat had a way of storing food for herself, didn't she?"

Sooren said, "What's the other story?"

Martha told them that when they were living in Monnetier-Mornex, France, her life was so busy that she had to knock herself out to attend to all her chores and responsibilities. Thus, Martha always fed Mao and Sandy in a rush and dashed out, either to drive Haroot or Sylvia to school, or take her mother and mother-in-law to see different doctors. For three consecutive days, she fed the animals in their appropriate dishes without bothering to wash the dishes. The third day, when Martha arrived home carrying a load of groceries, she found that Mao had peed in his dish. Martha said that she sat down in the kitchen chair and held her tummy as she laughed like mad.

"Yes," she said, "Mao was trying to give me a hint, saying that his feeding dish was disgusting and was no better than a litter box."

Bizet asked, "You say that Mao and Sandy were well-traveled pets, but you don't mention Mei."

"Yes, I know. Unfortunately, when we moved to France from Tehran at the beginning of the Iranian Revolution, she died there from spleen cancer."

Chapter 56

What Became of Shoonik?

Martha suddenly thought of her loyal dog. "I wonder where Shoonik could be. I hope the guards didn't entrap him the day they arrested us."

Sooren shook his head. "Don't worry. He is way too fast for any human being to be able to catch him. I assure you that he is trying to find a way to free us from this miserable dungeon."

Sooren added that they had not heard the last of that noble dog. Yes, indeed, he made them believe that Shoonik could be up to something.

Martha, now feeling relieved, looked pleased. Then, contemplating a different subject, she asked, "One thing baffles me, Uncle Sooren. I really can't fathom how evil can exist on Planet Heaven. Remember, back on Earth, we were taught that there is hell, whose ruler is the devil, where all the evildoers go?"

"Yes, I remember. I guess God believes in forgiveness. He lets them exist on Planet Heaven and gives them a chance to change."

"I get it. Then once they change their ways, He allows them to come to the open and lead a normal life, right?"

"Yes, I believe so."

He then reminded Martha of the Reform Center on Planet Heaven, where souls are sent to cleanse themselves of their evil deeds. Of course, the length of their stay at that institution depended on the magnitude of their evil actions committed both during their lifespan as well as on Planet Heaven, Sooren explained.

Martha asked, "Who runs the Reform Center?"

"Archangel Michael."

Chapter 57

Downheartedness

One morning Martha found herself feeling terribly disheartened. Even Bizet's new and cheerful composition of the day did nothing to brighten her spirits. She was terribly depressed and dying to escape into the bright, sunny environment of Planet Heaven. Indeed, she desired to enjoy the heavenly atmosphere of her new homeland. Martha had really had enough of that musty-smelling, dismal, dark cell. How long could she tolerate that stale atmosphere? No matter how hard Bizet and her uncle tried to cheer her up, they failed. What's more, Martha missed her parents and brothers badly. She told herself, *despite the fact that I have been here for a short while, I have reached the end of my patience. How about poor Bizet, who has tolerated the gloomy air of this prison for two centuries?*

As Martha quietly sat in the cell lost in her thoughts, she began pondering about her own past behavior on Earth. She thought most probably the reason why she had been imprisoned was because of her past sins, such as her act of trying to bring about the miscarriage of her baby, Haroot! She was sure that she could be blamed for many other wrongdoings. Martha told herself that if only she had been able to save Georges Bizet from his bondage, probably God would have forgiven her. However, there was nothing she could do about it at the present time. She was totally lost and had no idea what was in store for them all.

Martha suddenly remembered how on Earth, both during her youth and the last few years of her life, she had occasionally been confronted by certain dilemmas. Normally during such difficulties, Martha had turned to God, and He had always come to her rescue. This thought immediately soothed her spirits. Martha took a deep breath and knelt on the cold prison floor.

As soon as she began praying to God and asking Him for help, a thought flashed in her mind, as if God was speaking to her. Martha thought, *Didn't my uncle and I change Bizet's life by relieving him of his solitude?*

Martha immediately stood to her feet and began smiling. Her mood had completely changed. She was no longer depressed. Martha knew that her prayer already had been answered by that revelation. Thus, once again, she became her normal happy self, which in turn brightened up her uncle's and Bizet's mood. It felt for them all that the sun had begun shining in the dark, musty dungeon.

Sooren smiled and said, "Everything is good, isn't it? I have a feeling that something pleasant will soon happen to us."

"Yes, Uncle. I think so too."

"I hope so!" Bizet said and began singing his latest joyful composition.

Chapter 58

A Bright Light in the Darkness

Bizet's masculine, operatic voice flooded the air in the somber cellar, rendering Martha and Sooren happy. Martha sat on the floor feeling relaxed. Her head began nodding, while her eyelids felt as heavy as a truckload of cement bricks. Meanwhile, she felt as weightless as vapor permeating the stale air of the basement. Bizet, noticing Martha's sudden shift of mood, began singing even louder.

Within seconds, Martha fell asleep.

In her sound and deep slumber, she dreamed of a round, flat, and rubbery-looking bird. It was the size of the palm of a man's hand. Its circular, friendly eyes and little leaf like wings made it resemble a small turtle with no shell.

The bird, in Martha's dream, began speaking like a real person. It said, "I am bringing you good news. Wake up now."

Martha suddenly awakened with a start at the sound of the cell door flying open with a screeching groan. She immediately sat up like a straight metallic pillar in the unfriendly den as her heart drummed wildly.

The first thought that popped into her mind was that the guards probably were back to torture them. Otherwise, why would they come in again, after having already been there to give them their scanty ration of food? Besides, it was neither breakfast, lunch, nor dinnertime. Maybe they had come to transport them all to a prison even more miserable than the present one.

Martha told herself she did not care one way or the other. All she knew was that she was in no mood to see the miserable faces of the unfriendly guards. But did she have a choice? Meanwhile, Martha realized that she missed Shoonik badly. She remembered being in Iran on Earth as a little girl. At least for the moment, the thought of the old days took her mind off her glum situation.

Then something magical took place, which stunned all three prisoners. The dark cellar suddenly altered into a dazzling, bright dwelling. It felt like the dingy cellar had miraculously been illuminated by a gigantic projector light.

The spellbound detainees immediately jumped to their feet like bouncing springs. *This can't be!* Martha thought, dazed. *What is happening?* Having grown so accustomed to darkness, the three found the unexpected illumination completely confused their senses.

Chapter 59

Can It Be Real?

It took Martha quite a while to emerge out of her stupor. And, as she stood in her cell dumbstruck and speechless, she felt a dog hopping up and down. It looked like he was trying to reach her face and lick it. Shading her eyes from the blinding glare, she looked down and noticed that the dog was none other than her beloved Shoonik.

"Oh, dear Shoonik. My precious Shoonik! It's you! Uncle Sooren was right to think that you were up to something!"

Sooren yelled, "You're back! You're back, our sweet and beloved Shoonik!"

Bizet, too, sprang up and called out with great excitement, "So, this is the famous Shoonik!"

Shoonik stuck his ears back, the way dogs do when they are happy, and sprang up on his hind legs, this time to reach Bizet's face and lick it. As all this was happening, they suddenly noticed a smiling angel in a long, white robe walking toward them. He moved gracefully, stretching his hand to shake hands with all three of them. Then he walked back up the winding staircase, opened the cell door, and set them free.

As the three of them stared flabbergasted at the glowing angel, he smiled at them lovingly. "I'm Michael," he introduced himself, as he beckoned them out of the dungeon.

Uncle Sooren bowed to him with great respect and said, "Archangel Michel, you've found us!"

"Yes, my son. I must say that this special dog, whomever he belongs to, is such a jewel."

Martha said, "Yes, my lord, he indeed is." Then, realizing that there were no signs of the nasty guards, she asked, "Could you kindly fill us in as to what has happened?"

"First, before I go on telling you about everything, let me thank you two for your endeavor in looking for our unfortunate brother, Georges Bizet. I assure you that if it were not for you, he might have been imprisoned in this cell indefinitely."

Archangel Michael went on to explain that Shoonik, after seemingly searching for a long time, ended up at the Reform Center. He went straight to the angel, who knows how to communicate with animals, and relayed that the composer Georges Bizet was imprisoned at Escudier's boarding house, along with Martha, and her uncle, Sooren.

Archangel Michael said, "Since reform of the evildoers is my responsibility, I decided to come in person and rescue you all." He beamed contentedly. "I am so impressed with Shoonik! He cleverly led me here."

Martha smiled proudly to hear her dog praised by a holy figure such as Archangel Michael.

Chapter 60

What's Next?

"You are free. Hurry up. Go and spend some time with your family members," urged the archangel. "But please don't forget that Georges Bizet is going to need your help."

Sooren interjected, "Not to worry, my lord. We will take good care of him."

Martha said, "Of course we will look after him. He has become like kin to us."

The archangel nodded approvingly and said, "Thank you. I have no doubt about it." He sighed and continued, "Although we all very well knew that he has been living on Planet Heaven for centuries, we were unaware that he has been locked up all that while."

Martha interjected, "How come?"

The archangel said, "When people pray and ask for help, the heavenly authorities become aware of their whereabouts. Unfortunately, Bizet never reached out for help. He suffered in silence."

Archangel Michael stared at Martha and went on, "Besides, the second problem is the existence of bureaucracy on Planet Heaven, which creates big problems. From now on I am going to do everything in my power to eliminate it."

Martha nodded approvingly and said, "Georges has no idea about how to get around on Planet Heaven." She smiled and carried on. "I assure you that we will do everything in our power to help him find a new life for himself."

"Thank you. I'm happy Georges has such nice friends."

Then, in a flash of light, Archangel Michael was gone.

Sooren looked at Martha and Bizet thoughtfully and said, "Let's hope that Escudier will soon repent at the Reform Center and return to his boarding house as a normal and kind human being."

Martha and Bizet nodded, as they walked through the long corridor into the lobby. They noticed a multitude of peaceful people roaming there, and a pretty young African American woman had replaced Escudier at the reception desk. The smiling administrator waved at Martha and Sooren, and as they were about to step out of the door, she called out, "Have a good day!"

Outside, Bizet was speechless at the sight of the luscious green garden, the laughing and playful children, dogs and cats, giraffes, flamingos, and some piglets meandering peacefully. The air was so pleasant and extremely soothing to him. Bizet breathed deeply and uttered, "Oh, what lovely fresh air! Is this possible at all?"

Martha and Sooren were delighted to see Bizet so mesmerized by the bright and welcoming outdoor environment of Planet Heaven. They, too, felt a bit dazed to be outside again.

Bizet beamed with joy as he tried to take in everything. Presently, he composed himself and simply followed his friends. "I'm truly stunned by this incredible sense of freedom. Is this really true? Tell me I'm not dreaming!" He then shook his head with disbelief and added, "By the way, Sooren, I have no idea who Archangel Michael is."

Sooren told them the story about Archangel Michael as written in the Bible which he had studied in Sunday school during his teenage years. He recounted, "According to the book of Revelation, a war broke out between Heaven and the devil and his wicked army. Archangel Michael and his benevolent angels defeated Satan and threw the devil and his army out of Heaven."

Sooren further explained to Bizet that right from the start, God had decided that Michael should be responsible for helping people to reform. In other words, he was and still is responsible for eliminating evil from Planet Heaven.

Martha asked, "What do you think will happen to Escudier, Gounod, and their men?"

"As you know, they are already at the Reform Center," Sooren said. He went on to say that unfortunately, he had no idea about the programs being administered at that organization. All he knew was that the evildoers were taught how to turn into compassionate, spiritual, and charitable characters.

Martha said, "I am sure they will make Gounod return all the musical compositions that he made Bizet write for him during the time Bizet was imprisoned at Escudier's cell."

"Yes," Sooren cut in. "Gounod pretended that they were his own work and poor Bizet had no choice but to be obedient."

Chapter 61

Back to Business

As they walked toward the Champs-Élysées, Martha had no idea what was in store for her. Who was she destined to see? Where was she supposed to live? Maybe with her family in Iran? Besides, Martha had no idea what she really wished to do. Back on planet Earth, she had been an author. What were the possibilities for an author on Planet Heaven?

Sooren looked at her quizzically. "Anything wrong?" he asked.

"I was just wondering about my future situation here on Planet Heaven. Will I be choosing an occupation of my choice, or will somebody assign me a duty?"

"I think when you refer to the appropriate authorities concerning life upon this planet, you can either make a suggestion about what you wish to do, or ask them about some possibilities for a person with your characteristics," Sooren said.

"Do you know whom I could turn to?'

"The best thing to do would be to visit the Department of Labor, either in person or by logging onto their site on the Internet."

Bizet, still overwhelmed by the outdoor life and the beautiful streets of Paris bubbling with energy, could not help but overhear.

"I was actually going to ask you, Martha, if you would like to be my manager."

"Are you serious? Me, the real unprofessional in the field of music? If you were to talk about writing, it would be a different matter."

He looked at Martha with affection and smiled. "You know, Martha, you were so thoughtful and kind in wanting to find me. I think you are an interesting and talented person. I wish you would consider my offer. I think together we can be very fruitful."

Martha smiled in agreement. "Yes, you are so right. Fortunately, I really love your music. Indeed, I couldn't ask for a better occupation than managing your priceless work. I could, for example, find the right recording company to produce your compositions. I could organize concerts…"

Bizet asked, "How would you go about doing that, as a novice on Planet Heaven?"

Sooren wore a crooked smile on his face, as he looked confidently at his niece. He uttered, "She can go online and search, just the way she did on Earth. Don't worry; she is a professional."

"Whatever you two say. And please note that I trust you both immensely. I personally know nothing about…that thing. The modern machine."

"You mean the computer?" Martha asked.

"Yes. I was never exposed to that technology during my lifetime." He took on a serious look. "I haven't even been lucky enough to have walked around Planet Heaven, which I'm certain is much more advanced than Earth."

"How could you have? Poor you!" Martha said.

"That's why I beg you to help me," Bizet pleaded.

Martha patted Bizet on the shoulder and uttered, "Of course, I could help you. But on one condition: that I could be allowed to get involved in some other responsibilities on my free time. For, besides being helpful to you, I could probably assist another person as well."

Chapter 62

Teaching Children to be Humble

Presently, Martha, Sooren, and Georges Bizet arrived on the majestic and glorious Champs-Élysées. Bizet was taken aback by the beauty. He also was shocked to see all those cars zooming about like some kind of strange machines. He was surprised that there were no horses! Martha explained to him how those machines operated and on what they ran.

As they jaunted along the pleasant and elegant Parisian streets, Martha told Bizet and Sooren that one of the things she would love to do would be to help children on Earth to become more compassionate, charitable, and modest. She added that in her opinion, youngsters were very much spoiled by their parents. Martha thought that they received way too many gifts and material objects, much more than they really needed. Martha also thought that children, especially in the Western countries in general, were unaware about how badly, for example, kids in Africa suffered from hunger and want of ordinary necessities of life.

Martha brought up her own grandchildren as an example. She talked about the days when she and Zaven had to look after their three grandchildren while Haroot and his wife, Jenik, traveled abroad. The children would often ask their grandparents to get them certain toys and fun objects. Normally, those items were quite costly. Their grandchildren had no notion of things either being expensive or affordable. Their parents had provided them with almost everything they wished to have.

Martha, who as a child had experienced hardship after her father's death, thought it would be wise to teach them a bit of economy. She decided to give them each five dollars as pocket money every time they asked for a toy. Martha wanted to see how they would manage their wishes with such little money.

The day Martha took the kids to a toy store, they had such a fun time running from shelf to shelf, trying to figure out how to spend their money cleverly. Fortunately, there were so many small knickknacks that could be purchased at low cost. Thus, they had to think hard and calculate what they could afford to buy with their pocket money. Many years later, the three grandchildren told Martha that it was the best experience they had ever gone through as children. Consequently, when they got older, they told their grandmother that despite all the nice things and gifts that they received from their parents, buying toys with their pocket money was the most amusing thing they had done during their childhood. Yes, indeed, they did cherish the challenge of managing their meager budgets.

"I think in the modern world, most children are like my grandchildren, and they need to be aware of their privileged lives," Martha concluded. "That's why I would like to be able to teach children of Earth the sense of charity, humility, unselfishness, and compassion."

Sooren nodded approvingly and said, "Well-brought-up children will form a fair and kinder world. I so much agree with your decision."

Bizet also showed his support by adding, "I can also help you in preparing their ears for music. People who occupy their lives with music are normally fine human beings."

Chapter 63

The Eighth of April

As the three were busy talking, with Shoonik sitting by their side, Sooren took out his iPhone and checked it for new messages. He said, "Do you two have any idea about the date today?"

Bizet, who had been locked up for two and a half centuries and had completely lost track of time, shook his head. "I have to get used to dates and all," he said.

Martha looked at her uncle, smiling, and observed, "You can see the date on your iPhone, can't you? Otherwise, you, too, wouldn't know anything about the date!"

"Exactly, my dear. However, today is the eighth of April."

"Is it really? Oh my God, we got our freedom back on Haroot's birthday. How exciting!"

Bizet asked, "Oh yes? How old is he?"

"Haroot is fifty-two today," Martha answered, her eyes gleaming with joy.

"Congratulations!" Bizet and Sooren echoed in unison.

Martha thanked them as Bizet asked, "Was he born in Iran?"

"No," she answered. "He was born in Garmisch, Germany."

Martha explained how the night Haroot was born, she had to give birth alone at the hospital. Zaven had brought his wife by a taxi to the hospital from Oberammergau, where they worked and lived, and the night nurse had not allowed him to stay with Martha.

"I think that it was an experience that not many women would like to go through," she uttered, shaking her head.

Both men agreed. They could guess how dismayed Martha must have felt. Martha appreciated their compassion toward her, and as she looked at them beamingly, her mind revolved around her family on Earth. Turning to her loving companions, she said dreamily, "I wonder what plans they all have for Haroot's birthday tonight!"

Sooren answered, "Whatever they do, I'm sure they'll be missing you a lot."

Martha nodded and heaved a sigh. "I wish I were with them. I would have danced with Haroot. Then Alain, my eighteen-year-old grandson, would cut in to dance with me. Haroot's little dog, Jackson, would stand on his hind legs and try to dance with me as well. He always loved to dance with the family members when Haroot started playing his joyful repertoire of pop music."

"That's fantastic!" Bizet said. "I can tell what a warm family you have. I, personally, never had such pleasures when I was on Earth. Unfortunately, my warm relationship with my wife was short-lived. She found a lover while I was ill." Bizet looked down at his black, old-fashioned shoes, bit his lip, and continued. "Unfortunately, her behavior pushed me into finding a mistress as well." He sighed. "No, I can't claim having had a nice life on Earth."

Martha said, "But I'm sure you must have some happy memories from your past life!"

"Yes, you're right. The only time I enjoyed myself on Earth was when I composed my music. The moment I would begin to create an opera, I would step into a different realm of emotional life, which was magical. Really; it was the best feeling!"

"I know how fun it is when you immerse yourself into your creative world. I felt the same way when I wrote. However, for me, nothing gives me more pleasure than, for example, spending some nice and rich moments with my uncle, as well as good friends. I used to have that kind of a relationship with my lovely Sylvia. Also with Haroot, Zaven, Jenik, and the rest of my family members, not to mention my brothers and sister."

Bizet nodded in agreement. "Sylvia is your daughter, right?"

"Yes, she is, and I considered her my best friend. I miss her so much!"

"Tell me, where was she born? In Germany, like Haroot?"

"No, she was born in Tehran, but she was not even two when we left Tehran to live in Germany."

While the three heavenly friends were eagerly conversing, Martha's attention was drawn to a slim, dark-haired fellow staring at her. She racked her memory to remember the man's face.

Who is he, dear Lord? Why does his face look so familiar?

Definitely, there was something in his looks that made him appear as an acquaintance, especially because he was smiling so warmly at Martha. It seemed like he knew her.

Oh yes, I know, Martha told herself. *There is something about him that makes me think of Zaven and Haroot.*

She turned to Sooren and asked, "Uncle, look at that man standing a few steps away by the tree and gazing at me."

"Yes," Sooren said. "You are talking about that chap on the sidewalk with brown drowsy eyes, a crooked smile, nicely trimmed goatee, and dark, straight hair. Aren't you?"

"Yes, that good-looking guy over there."

"No, I don't think I know him," Sooren said, shaking his head.

Martha closed her eyes and tried to recall if Zaven might have had a friend or a relative whom she had met once, a while back. On the other hand, she thought, *Maybe a picture of a relative…*And, sure enough, she suddenly remembered something…

Martha envisaged a large photo of the same man perched on their side table in the dining room.

"Uncle, I think I know. This guy is Zaven's maternal grandfather, Boris, who was assassinated by a Communist sympathizer when Zaven was three years old."

Chapter 64

What a Coincidence

Martha jumped to her feet and ran toward the stranger. She stretched her hand to shake his and uttered, "If I'm not mistaken, you must be Grandfather Boris. Am I right?"

He smiled and hugged Martha. "Yes, you are right. And I know that you are Martha, my grandson's wife."

Martha screeched with excitement. She was overjoyed to meet the legendary Boris on Planet Heaven. She asked Boris bashfully, "How do you know me? You had passed away many, many years back, before I married Zaven. Thus, we never met."

"Well, my dear, I had a chance to travel to Earth on your wedding day and be one of the many spirit guests at your wedding. Tell me, did you guess who I was through my pictures that you had seen on Earth?"

"Yes, Boris. Can I call you Boris?"

"By all means!" he stressed.

"Oh, dear Boris, I am delighted to meet you in person."

Then, Martha introduced Boris to Sooren and Georges Bizet, as they began walking on the Champs-Élysées.

Boris decided to join the group on their trip to Iran. Bizet, meanwhile, could not believe he would be visiting Iran, the land of Omar Khayyam, Sa'di, and Ferdowsi, the world-renowned poets. He always thought of them as being special artists who spoke about love, wine, and a dream world that Bizet adored.

Presently, they were proceeding toward the direction of the Swiss border, when Sooren heard his iPhone buzz.

"This could be a message from one of our family members," he said, smiling with pleasure. He could hardly wait to get home and be with all his loved ones.

Martha rushed to her uncle's side to find out what the news was.

Sooren's face beamed brightly as he uttered, "Good news, Martha! Zaven arrived this very minute at your parent's house."

"Oh, you are talking about my grandson?" Boris said eagerly.

"Yes, Boris, we are talking about my darling husband, your grandson," Martha said as she hopped up and down with joy like a young girl. "He will be so happy to see you. We will keep it as a surprise for him."

"Yes, yes. Let's do that," Sooren uttered.

Bizet looked perplexed. He had no idea what to expect in an Armenian home when he finally arrived in Tehran. He smiled and asked, "Do you drink any alcohol in your households?"

"Oh yes," Martha responded enthusiastically. "Our favorite beverage, aside from water, is vodka."

"I personally love wine," Bizet said. "Especially French wine, which I've missed tremendously all these centuries."

Sooren laughed mischievously and said, "Don't you worry. You will have your special French wine, too."

Martha began laughing uncontrollably and retorted, "If you think French wine is good, wait until you drink Jesus's wine. I promise you that you will immediately begin composing even more superb musical chefs d'oeuvre."

Martha thought that after arriving home to visit her family members and welcome Zaven, she and Sooren, with Shoonik's help, could take Bizet and Zaven to meet Jesus on a Tuesday, his reception day. Indeed, she could not wait to accompany her husband to Heaven. She was eager to hear Zaven holding interesting conversations with Jesus, maybe even with Moses.

Chapter 65

The Reason Why Boris was Assassinated

George Bizet asked, "Boris, Martha told us that you were murdered by a Communist sympathizer. Can you tell us what happened?"

He swallowed hard, examined their faces one by one, and answered, looking glum. "Oh, I don't like to remember that horrible incident. The day I was shot dead, I was traveling from Tehran to Tabriz to join my wife and grandson."

He said that he adored his three-year-old grandson, Zaven, whom he had not seen for a month because of traveling on business. Martha remembered the photograph of three-year-old Zaven with his handsome grandfather and the loving look on the man's face as he stared at little Zaven.

Boris continued, "Actually, the guy who shot me pretended to be a good friend of mine."

Martha covered her mouth with her hand and exclaimed, "I can't believe it! How can somebody in their right mind shoot a friend because of some political ideas?"

"I used to be quite hostile to the Communist system, and I publicly admitted it"

"Why?" Bizet inquired. "Can you tell us a bit about that?"

Boris explained to Bizet that he had been born in Armenia and raised in Russia by his mother. Boris's father died when he was a little boy. Then, he said, when he grew up and finished his studies, he started his own confectionary business.

"I was doing so well, until the Communist regime took over Russia and confiscated my business and everything else that I had."

Boris said that he hated the Communists. To him, they were worse than Fascists.

Sooren asked him, "How did you end up in Iran?"

He smiled, thinking about those days, and answered, "The Persian embassy in Moscow was selling their country's citizenship to Russians who wished to get away from the Communist systems. I got my mother and my six-year-old daughter Persian passports and got out of the Soviet Union."

"Very interesting," Bizet said. "How about your wife?"

"My wife, Natasha, a Russian, joined the Red Army and abandoned me and our little girl."

"That's cruel!" Sooren exclaimed. "What kind of mother would do such a thing?"

"Well," Boris croaked, appearing very disturbed. "She was very selfish. Yes, she broke my heart." He sighed. "Natasha evaporated into thin air. No matter how much I searched for her, she was nowhere to be found."

Bizet said, "Didn't you say that the day you got shot, you were on your way home to see your wife and your grandson?" He waited awhile for Boris to answer him. When Boris stared away instead of answering, Bizet smiled and added, "Did Natasha finally return to you?"

"No, she didn't," he said, "But the woman in question was my second wife, whom I married in Persia."

He went to say that his daughter and her husband were away in Europe when Boris was killed and that his wife was taking care of their grandson.

Martha interjected, turning to Sooren and Bizet, "And of course, we should remember that Zaven's mother was Natasha's daughter. Boris's second wife, Elena, did not bear any children for Boris." Then she addressed Boris. "Tell me, have you met with both your wives here?"

"Yes, I have."

"How do you handle having two wives on Planet Heaven?"

Boris gave Martha a friendly smile and responded, "I have no feelings for either one. In fact, they have become good friends with each other."

Bizet asked, "You said your friend killed you, didn't you?"

"Yes. You want to know why my friend shot me dead, don't you?"

"Right."

Boris explained that his friend was a hot-blooded Communist. He hated the fact that Boris was so much opposed to the Soviet regime—to the point that he shot him in rage.

Bizet asked Boris, "Tell me—have you seen your killer?"

Boris smiled. "No, I haven't had the honor yet."

Chapter 66

The Holy E-mail

Sooren's cell phone began to ring, startling him and Martha. Martha exclaimed, "What's up now? We already know that Zaven has arrived on Planet Heaven. I hope he is all right!"

"Yes," Sooren answered, before he answered the call. "I'm one hundred percent sure Zaven is fine. Don't worry at all. Maybe it's him trying to reach you."

They stopped walking as the latter answered the call. "Hello, Sooren speaking," he shouted amid the deafening noises of the busy street.

Martha, beholding her uncle's pensive appearance, enquired anxiously, "Anything wrong, Uncle?"

"No, no," Sooren responded. "The automated voice message simply stated I should check my e-mail for an important message."

"Then, hurry up, Uncle. What are you waiting for?"

Martha tried to peek nosily over Sooren's shoulder as her uncle examined his most recent e-mails. One message was blinking like a burning bush. Sooren blushed as his eyebrows arched, almost hitting his hairline.

"What's going on?" Martha asked.

Sooren's face radiated as he swayed his head from side to side with astonishment. "Lucky woman! You have another e-mail, but this time it is very special. Yes, I tell you, there are not many people who receive a notice from God's office."

"Oh, come on. Be serious, please," Martha said, thinking her uncle was trying to tease her.

"I am serious!" Sooren protested and passed the iPhone over to Martha. "Go on—read it yourself."

Martha grabbed the electronic device with trembling hands as her whole body began to shake. She had no idea whether she should be happy or scared to have received a message from the Almighty. Had she done anything wrong by looking for Georges Bizet? Had she interfered in God's affairs?

As Martha started to read the message, her eardrums almost exploded with her loud heartbeat. She closed her eyes to compose herself, took a deep breath, and then glued her eyes on the text of the e-mail. It read:

Re: Finding and Saving Georges Bizet
Dear Martha,

I understand you have discovered Georges Bizet's prison and have saved him from the clutches of evil. I commend you, your uncle, and your dog in this brave endeavor. Therefore, I would very much like for all of you to appear at My court next Monday and tell Me about everything in detail. Your action tells Me that we all have to work hard against the existence of evil on Planet Heaven.

*Looking forward to seeing you at ten in the morning
on Monday.
Affectionately,
Your Heavenly Father*

Martha patted Shoonik's head as her face turned totally red, hot, and sweaty with extreme exhilaration. "Wow! Can you imagine?" She yelled at the top of her voice as pedestrians stared at her. "Who would think I would be summoned to the Almighty's court?"

Shoonik began making small happy noises, understanding the situation quite well.

"Lucky girl!" Bizet and Sooren uttered in unison. Bizet continued, "I can't wait to hear all about it next week after your important visit."

Chapter 67

Another Call

The cell phone rang again. They all stopped talking. Each time there was a call or an e-mail, they knew that there was something important happening. However, what could be more important than a message from the Almighty?

Ring, ring. The iPhone kept echoing in the air, despite the noisy street.

"Come on; answer it already!" Martha almost yelled at Sooren.

He looked at the screen of his iPhone and announced, "Here, take it. It is for you, Martha."

Martha grabbed the iPhone and answered, "Hello? Hello, Martha speaking."

"Oh, my lovely Martha! I can't believe I'm hearing your sweet voice!"

"Oh my Lord! I know this voice. Who is it really?"

"Martha, don't you recognize me? Come on—say something. I'm dying to talk with you!" the voice protested.

Martha stood quiet for a second in contemplation and then uttered, "Goodness! Goodness, I couldn't imagine that you would call."

"My love, I miss you. I so much miss you. When are you going to come home? It seems you are having a grand time without me."

"Oh, Zaven! Zaven, stop. I can't wait to get home to see you."

Sooren smiled lovingly. He could feel his niece's joy over hearing her husband's voice.

Zaven asked, "Do you think you will arrive home tonight?"

Martha turned to her uncle and asked, "What shall I tell him? Are we going to be home tonight?"

"Yes," Sooren answered. "But very late."

Martha relayed the news about their late arrival and then explained to Zaven about receiving a letter from the Almighty's office concerning her meeting with Him on Monday.

He yelled with excitement. "That's wonderful! That's my wife! I always knew that you were adventurous and exciting. I am not surprised for your success on Planet Heaven."

Martha felt uneasy about all the praise bestowed on her by her husband. She thought that she had simply been lucky. Yes, Martha thought that she was indeed fortunate to be noticed by God's office.

"You know what, Martha?" Zaven's voice echoed in Martha's ears like an English horn.

"What?"

"You'll be surprised to know that I've bought us a red 1960s Cadillac. I know how much you like the color."

Martha couldn't believe her ears. It was the same flamboyant, flashy, and exciting Zaven as he used to be on Earth until the day she died. He had hardly arrived on Planet Heaven, and he was already hard at work to continue living his earthly life.

"How exciting," Martha said. "Red! Yes, my favorite color. That reminds me—as soon as I begin my normal life, I will start buying myself some red clothing."

She was well aware that neither Zaven nor any of her family members had any idea what she and Sooren had gone through within the period of her stay on Planet Heaven.

"I'll drive you to your meeting in our new car," Zaven added.

"No, it doesn't work that way." She explained to him about those special fast-paced escalators that led to where she had met Jesus.

"I see," he said.

Martha, whose heart suddenly overflowed with love for her husband, smiled warmly and told him, "Zaven, I want you to know that when we go to the Almighty's office, I would like to take Uncle Sooren along."

"Yes, of course!" Zaven exclaimed.

Martha smiled mischievously and asked, "Tell me—did you finally throw those horrid yellow boots away?"

He laughed before answering, "Actually, I arrived on Planet Heaven in my precious yellow boots!"

About the Author

An American Armenian born in Iran, Armineh Helen Ohanian was published author already at age fifteen. Armineh is the author of three novels, and a Children storybook series called *the Talking Animals*. Her book, *"The Apple Tree Blossoms* in the Fall" is a highly acclaimed creative memoir. This book earned honorable mention in the category of biography and autobiography at the 2014 LA Book Festival. In 2012, Armineh was invited to Oxford University in the United Kingdom to hold a book signing and talk about her memoir during the university's International Women's Day celebrations. Armineh has lived in Europe and the United States since 1962. Presently, she lives in Westhampton, New York, with her husband and three cats. She is passionate about writing, reading, playing tennis, and driving sports cars.

Made in the USA
Middletown, DE
08 August 2015